The Blood King Legacy

(Matt Drake #19)

By

David Leadbeater

Thriller, adventure, action, mystery, suspense,
archaeological, military, historical

Other Books by David Leadbeater:

The Matt Drake Series
A constantly evolving, action-packed romp based in the
escapist action-adventure genre:

The Bones of Odin (Matt Drake #1)
The Blood King Conspiracy (Matt Drake #2)
The Gates of Hell (Matt Drake 3)
The Tomb of the Gods (Matt Drake #4)
Brothers in Arms (Matt Drake #5)
The Swords of Babylon (Matt Drake #6)
Blood Vengeance (Matt Drake #7)
Last Man Standing (Matt Drake #8)
The Plagues of Pandora (Matt Drake #9)
The Lost Kingdom (Matt Drake #10)
The Ghost Ships of Arizona (Matt Drake #11)
The Last Bazaar (Matt Drake #12)
The Edge of Armageddon (Matt Drake #13)
The Treasures of Saint Germain (Matt Drake #14)
Inca Kings (Matt Drake #15)
The Four Corners of the Earth (Matt Drake #16)
The Seven Seals of Egypt (Matt Drake #17)
Weapons of the Gods (Matt Drake #18)

The Alicia Myles Series
Aztec Gold (Alicia Myles #1)
Crusader's Gold (Alicia Myles #2)
Caribbean Gold (Alicia Myles #3)

The Torsten Dahl Thriller Series
Stand Your Ground (Dahl Thriller #1)

All genuine comments are very welcome at:

davidleadbeater2011@hotmail.co.uk

Twitter: @dleadbeater2011

Visit David's website for the latest news and information:
davidleadbeater.com

The Blood King Legacy

CHAPTER ONE

Greer and Archer sat inside a rented car outside the Arm Premier in Cherepovets, Russia, watching the hotel's well-lit front door. The hotel radiated amber from its twenty-three front windows, its angular eastern wing, and its central entryway. It looked homely, well-appointed and proficient. Above, a starless backdrop of pitch-black sky hung low.

Greer turned to Archer, taking his eyes off the door. "How long do you think we'll be here, mate?"

Archer sported a thick, pointed beard that wagged when he spoke. "Watching this guy? I'm not sure. Until he leaves Russia, I guess."

Greer watched the beard move up and down, mesmerized. "But there's nothing happening here, mate."

"It's a favor for Cambridge," Archer said. "He asks, you do it. You know how it goes. There's no downside to being owed a favor by an SAS captain."

"Aye, I guess you're right. But Cherepovets? I'm freezing my nuts off out here."

"Yeah, it's cold," Archer agreed. "But nothing compared to the ice fields to the east. I wonder why he keeps heading over there?"

Greer shrugged, turning his gaze back toward the hotel. "Looking for something. Same as we all are."

Archer said nothing. Both men continued to watch the hotel façade. As the night deepened, one by one, the hotel room lights flicked off as its patrons went to sleep.

Greer yawned. "I'm gonna catch a few. Don't wake me unless a bloody war breaks out."

Archer watched his companion lie back. Within a minute he was out, his body trained to take rest when it could. It was Archer's first time working with Greer, and he didn't much like the guy, but the job should gain him some favors down the line and, truth be told, it was a doddle. Their assignment, a Russian youth, had done nothing except travel to a village about two hours distant and trudge through the ice fields that surrounded it. Maybe he was testing himself.

But Archer trusted Cambridge. And that was the clincher—the reason he was here. Most of the lads had heard the whispers—about a secret stash of weapons collected by an American-based Special Ops team being stored somewhere in London. *Weapons of the Gods,* some of them said. Sounded weird, but Archer had seen and heard a lot of weird in his time as an SAS soldier. He didn't question it much; just kept on going.

Back home, his wife and their eight-year-old daughter were waiting. He was due some leave after this—and looked forward to it. The adjustment to civilian life wouldn't be easy, but Archer was always happy to make it.

Another light clicked off in the hotel. Yorgi's light. Archer relaxed, but never stopped scanning the shadows. The third member of their team—a recent arrival—to Archer's satisfaction, was stationed near the back entrance.

"Webster?" He clicked the hand-held radio. "You there? How's it looking?"

"That I am," a broad Yorkshire voice came back. "It's all good here. Your mate asleep, is he?"

"Greer's no mate of mine, but he is asleep. Shall we prank him?"

"If it'll make you feel better."

"Yeah, Shaun, then let's prank him."

Archer knew that soldiers in a hot zone, even when the op was sluggish, took what light relief they could. Unrelenting pressure and tension wasn't good for body or mind. And Webster could prank with the best of them.

"Call her, Webster. You sure you can pull this off?"

"Hey man, I never met a hooker I couldn't charm the pants off in one minute flat."

Archer frowned. "I don't think you really understand that concept, mate."

"Whatever,"

Webster signed off for a few minutes. Archer paid careful attention to the passing vehicles, the patrons entering and leaving the hotel at this late hour, and the car park around him. Remote surveillance wasn't foolproof by any means, but much depended on the instinct of the watcher. And Archer's instincts were peerless. They had been watching Yorgi for over a week now. And, until two days ago, Archer hadn't feared for the Russian's safety.

But two days ago, something changed. Something big. It started with a general communique—a message from base that put the entire regiment on alert. Activity was spiking all along the terrorist communication network—the same way it had before 911, the same way it had before a dozen other horrendous events. Britain was waiting for something to happen.

Imminently.

Archer expected to be called back home. He knew the President of the United States was due to visit London. But Cambridge didn't contact him. The threat level always increased when heads of state came to visit. London could handle it. Archer had relaxed and continued the watch, at odds with Greer but knowing Webster was on his way to help.

That morning, as Yorgi departed on his daily sojourn to the remote village, Archer saw a black SUV emerge from an alley three blocks down. The sight struck him as unusual for several reasons. First, there were no large, blacked-out expensive vehicles like it around this part of Cherepovets. Second, it waited for Yorgi to pass even though it didn't have to. Third, it waited as Yorgi entered the nearby coffee shop as if watching. Fourth, the entire scene raised Archer's heckles. Something wasn't right.

The vehicle was Russian, registered to a business in Moscow. Archer's contacts discovered that the business was a front. The owner was anonymous. After that, Archer and

Greer combed the area, checking roads, alleys and streets, and even sweeping Yorgi's room while he was out. Nothing more happened—which left Archer in a state of uneasiness.

Maybe the SUV hadn't been watching Yorgi.

Could it be here for *them?* The British?

The radio crackled, side-lining his thoughts. Webster was laughing. "All set up for the morning, mate. She'll be ready when he pops in for his breakfast muffin. I guess he'll end up with more muffin than he bargained for."

Archer grinned. "All quiet back there?"

"Yeah, mate, as a grave."

"Maybe Yorgi will find what he's looking for tomorrow."

"In that ice field? What could he possibly be looking for out there?"

"Closure, is my guess," Archer said. "Why else would a man leave a tight-knit team to travel alone, to return to his godforsaken town of birth, and then plod through such a cold hell for days on end?"

"You don't think his team canned him?"

"His team love him," Archer affirmed. "They pulled in some mega favor to assign us to him."

"That's true. He's important to them."

"So we better watch his ass good."

"You think he's in danger?"

Archer shook his head in the darkness. "I can't say for sure, but I hope he finishes up soon, mate. With the news from London, the increase in terrorist activity, the President's visit, Team SPEAR in London too, and this, I'm wondering if we're about to get properly busy."

"Whatever happens," Webster said. "Whatever it takes."

"Stay alert," Archer said. "And watch your back. We watch each other's. And we hope Greer does the same."

"He will. He's Regiment."

Archer looked across at the sleeping man. "Then we'll be fine."

CHAPTER TWO

Yorgi sat on the edge of the lumpy bed and checked the time: 11.00 p.m. here meant that it was 9.00 p.m. there. *Perfect. I will speak to my friends before my final journey tomorrow.*

The hotel room was dark, so he reached over and flicked a lamp on. It illuminated a scarred desk, a small television and a bedside table. The carpet was threadbare. The walls were clean but worn. Yorgi didn't care. He wasn't here to sightsee.

He was here for one reason only.

To find closure both for himself, and his brothers and sister.

They died so long ago now he couldn't remember the date, but the intervening years had almost broken him. Recently, he'd told the story of his siblings' deaths for the first time, and the telling had reawakened a need he'd subdued for almost two decades. Yorgi had departed for Russia almost immediately, but he kept in touch with his friends because they were his only family now.

You kill your parents in cold blood, you learn to live with self-hatred.

But they deserved it. Every step of the way. They deserved it.

Yorgi swallowed half a bottle of water before wandering over to the window. He felt lonely. Lonelier even than when he'd languished inside the Russian prison—fighting for survival every day until Matt Drake came along. He wondered now if he should have accepted the team's offer and brought one of them with him. Maybe even Alicia. She might enjoy teasing and ribbing him, but her heart and her skillset were unquestionable. He trusted all of them with his life.

So why are you here alone?

To face the reckoning. He owed his long-dead brothers

5

and sister a debt, and he would pay it alone.

Yorgi slipped out his cell phone and made a call. The voice of the man that answered it made him feel better.

"Ey up? That you, mate?"

Yorgi smiled at the empty, dispassionate hotel room. "It is, my friend. How are you?"

"Fair to middling, pal. Fair to middling."

Yorgi had no idea what the Yorkshireman meant, but his tone was content. "No more wild adventures?"

"Not since the last." Drake laughed. "We're here in London cataloguing the weapons of the gods as they're stored away inside a special vault. Boring, but it gives us the downtime."

"And playtime," a female voice put in with a naughty chuckle. "How you doing, Yogi?"

The Russian had long since given up correcting the blonde. "I am almost . . . home."

"Good. We're missing you."

"What's happening there?" Torsten Dahl asked. Yorgi could envision him pulling the phone from Drake's hand and taking over.

"I spent a while tracking the final journey that my parents took us on. Then I found the spot where we were forced to enter the ice fields. Tomorrow, I will find where my brothers and sister died."

There was a heavy silence. Into it, Yorgi spoke his most heartfelt words. "I feel that I should be in that ice field too. I should have died there. Why did I survive?"

Now Mai's voice came down the line. "I do not know your particular pain, but I do know about parental and sibling loss. Yorgi, you cannot blame yourself. It is not your fault."

He knew that, but it made little difference. He changed the subject. "I should see you guys in a few days. Maybe I'll get to see those weapons."

Drake answered. "Doubtful, mate. We're almost done here. The President's coming to London tomorrow, making a speech at the new embassy. They want us to stay for that and then we're heading back to DC."

"Is he in danger?"

"Nah, it's just precautionary. Nutballs and clowns always surface around a presidential visit."

"Yeah," Alicia said. "And that's just his entourage."

Yorgi laughed. "It's good to hear you guys," he said. "It's been a lonely week or so."

"We'll see each other soon," Mai said. "Good luck tomorrow."

He spoke his goodbyes and signed off. As soon as he put the phone down, the loneliness returned, hurting like a hole in his heart. Again, he walked to the window. A light snowfall had started outside. He saw nothing untoward out there, although he had been put on alert a few days earlier when he saw the occupants of a large SUV watching him.

But why would anyone be tracking him here? He later decided he was being paranoid.

Yorgi had faced many threats in his life. From Russian crime bosses to Yakuza warriors and military-trained assassins. He had faced cannibals. But the horrors he would face tomorrow in that ice field—they worried him more than all the others put together. He wasn't sure he could outface them.

The team's confidence in him helped. He'd learned so much from them, and watching people like Mai and Alicia cope with their own issues whilst fighting on the right side shored up his own convictions.

Yorgi made ready for the morning, packing his rucksack and ensuring he had all the right provisions and cold weather gear. It would be one last enormous effort. It would be a culmination of a lifetime of fear, worry and hatred.

Yorgi climbed into bed, not expecting to sleep. The day after tomorrow couldn't come fast enough.

CHAPTER THREE

Out in the icy wilderness, he felt like a ghost. It was an odd sensation, accentuated by the nature of his quest. He left the car parked on the verge of a narrow, frozen road and entered the ice fields at the same point he'd done yesterday. He walked for three minutes, found the marker he'd left, and stopped. It was hard going. Every step was treacherous. His breath plumed before his face. His cheeks stung with the bitter cold. His eyelashes had gained a frosting. Yorgi tried not to breathe too deeply; unwilling to let the negative temperatures fill his lungs.

Hard-packed ice crunched under his boots. The skies above were dark gray and heavy. There was nothing cheery about this place. It felt like death. Slowly, he passed through the frosty reaching limbs of shrubs that somehow clung to meagre life. He climbed a short hill, slipping back almost as often as he moved forward. He slid down the other side.

A gully presented a ten-minute obstacle. Eventually he just ran and jumped, clearing it and rolling, coming up intact, panting and swearing despite the cold. He paused, down on one knee, surveying his surroundings. The bleak gray-white landscape stretched forever, dotted by desperate shrubs and thin, grasping trees. Nothing moved. The silence echoed inside his head.

Yorgi planted another journey marker and moved on. Nothing was familiar, but he knew where they were. He'd made the trek thousands of times in his head, and mapped it five times in seven days. He knew his siblings couldn't be too far from the road. They hadn't staggered around out here for more than fifteen or twenty minutes.

Yorgi knew that ice formed and thickened quickly. There was no chance that he would find or see the remotest sign of his siblings out here. But he would know the place when he found it. And then he could stand among them once again.

This is the place.

It hit him with startling clarity; so hard that he fell to his knees. Hard ice slammed his knee caps, the cold seeped through his thick clothing. They were here, all around him. Tears formed at the corners of his eyes and rolled down his face. So often he had imagined this moment. So often he had dreamed of what he would say or do when he got here.

But now he was speechless. He bowed his head and cried. It was all he could do not to flatten himself and cry into the ice, but some sense remained as he realized what that would do to his exposed skin. Yorgi had no strength, no will. All he could do was kneel as endless sobs wracked his body.

His four brothers and one sister lay under this ice. Their graves for eternity. But now *no more.* He hadn't made this quest to end it right here.

When he felt stronger, Yorgi looked up. The clearing had distinctive features; he remembered that. He'd seen them in the pre-dawn long ago before staggering away. You could see a pointed rise to the left, a stand of frozen shrubbery to the right. Yes, it was somewhat different now, but the features combined, and the rise and fall of the land, the craggy surface where they'd all fallen right in front of him—it all told him he'd found the right place.

A lifetime ago, Yorgi's four brothers and one sister were murdered by his parents; children abandoned because parents couldn't cope, couldn't afford to feed them, couldn't live with that pressure. Which hopes and dreams had died that day? What incredible futures had been snuffed out by the icy wastes, by a drastic, deplorable decision? The fates of hundreds of people had been changed in an instant— everyone his siblings might have met and loved, everyone they might have helped and changed. Who could say how they might have affected the world?

Yorgi rose, legs still shaking. He stood for a moment. When he was able, he set about marking the clearing. He'd purchased some advanced tech for this job. Several markers: two surface tracking chips and two more of the same that he could bury. Yorgi pulled out a foldable shovel and took some time to bury them. When, later, he made it to a place with network coverage, he would email the tracking data to his own account and Drake's too. When he was finished he took another look around.

It was so utterly silent. The graves of his brothers and sisters lay all around him, Yorgi knew not exactly where. But they were here. He could feel their presence. He remembered their laughter, their spirit.

And he remembered their total bewilderment on the night they died. Never believing that their parents would do this, refuting it until the very end. Yorgi had survived because he was the oldest, the strongest. He somehow managed to stagger to a safe place. He believed then that luck had saved him to claim revenge, and now to save them from this terrible, frozen eternity. They would be re-interred in the cheeriest place he could find. It was the best he could do for them now.

Yorgi began to feel the chill seeping through his protective clothing. All he wanted to do was to stay here all day, alongside his old friends, but the arctic chill forbade him. It was time to go. The trek back would raise his temperature and then the car journey would be easy. The hardest thing he'd ever done was almost over. He felt a terrible mix of sadness and joy, something he would have to come to terms with. It made his stomach churn.

The act of leaving was a terrible wrench. He turned away and couldn't do it. Returned once more. Wept again. Finally, feeling weak and cold, he followed the red markers back to the car, leaving his siblings alone once more.

With a promise.

I'll be back soon. As I promised long ago, I will save you.

Thirty minutes later, the car loomed out of a growing murk. A fog bank was drifting in but had held off just long enough for him to find the shelter he needed. In truth, he'd thought of that possibility and had left a tracker in the car, but nature's chance assistance was welcome.

Yorgi let out a pent-up breath and approached the car. He thumbed the key to open the trunk. He would shed some of the heavier clothing to make the drive back more comfortable. The big coat went in the back and then a couple of under-layers, exchanged for a warm thermal jacket. He changed his boots for sneakers. He rolled his shoulders to relieve some of the tension, wiped the icy residue of tears from his cheeks.

Distracted, he didn't see the movement of large figures behind him.

But he did hear the clicks of fingers on triggers as they approached.

Webster, Greer and Archer retraced their steps back to Yorgi's car. It had been a sobering, emotional few hours. They'd sat in silence, trying not to watch a man come to terms with some terrible past that they knew nothing about. They took turns surveying the area, guarding him, and making sure the path back to the car remained clear.

Finally, they made it back. Yorgi was to their right, just stepping out of the wastes and onto the main road. He trudged to his car. Their own vehicle was three hundred yards away, off road, in the opposite direction to which he should go. Greer had already set off to extract it. He would pick them up from here two minutes after Yorgi left.

Archer and Webster crouched in the meagre underbrush, wearing camouflage fatigues, watching as Yorgi shrugged out of his coat and changed his boots. Their weapons were holstered. Webster was blowing on his hands. Archer thought that their Russian sojourn might soon be over. Yorgi's mission had moved him, and he wanted to know the details, but he was also happy that, soon, they'd be moving on.

Webster tapped his arm. "See that? What the—"

Figures moved out of the murk on the far side of the road. They came from the arctic wastes. Archer counted five, six, seven, and more; all dressed in dark clothing; hulking, shadowy and carrying shotguns.

Carrying all manner of guns, he now saw. A real mish-mash.

Shit.

Archer drew and pointed his own weapon, a Sig Sauer P226, 9mm, as used by the Regiment far and wide, fitted with a twenty-round magazine. It was clear the new group were focused on Yorgi, weapons raised, so he didn't hesitate.

"This is what we came for," Webster muttered and opened fire.

Their bullets tore among the attackers. Several twisted and fell. Others swiveled toward the SAS men. Archer moved fast. He saw Yorgi spinning, a look of shock on his face. Archer raced toward him, still firing at the enemy.

The figures kept coming, emerging from the gloom. More now. At least fifteen. Four were on the floor, twitching. A bullet tore past him, another smashed into the ice close to his right foot. Webster was several yards to his left, drawing more fire. Still, he kept them busy, every bullet finding a target and bringing the enemy down.

Archer reached Yorgi. "Get in the car. Get in the *goddamn car.*"

Yorgi was fast, trained through years of association with the SPEAR team. Nevertheless, a bullet whipped through his jacket, snagging the arm and drawing a line of blood. The young Russian yelped.

Archer dragged him around the side of the car. "Get down!"

Behind the wheel, they had momentary cover. Archer peered around the trunk's open hatch, fired three more times. Three men fell. He changed the mag, shouting at Webster for cover. Webster leaned out and fired, drawing attention. Archer thought about Greer and thumbed his mic.

"We're under attack. Get here, now!"

No answer. Archer pushed Yorgi toward the rear passenger door, watched the man wrench it open. To his credit, he already had the ignition keys in his hand. Archer pushed him down along the back seat and took them from him. Webster cried out that he was changing mags, which prompted Archer back to the rear of the car.

A quick look. He saw ten men on the ground, but still the figures came. At least twenty more moving now. Bullets peppered the back of the car, shredding metal and shattering glass. Archer felt a blitz of debris pass right before his face. Sharp splinters entered his flesh.

He raised the Sig and fired, unable to miss amid the crowd that came at them. This was no time for finesse. Without pause, he emptied the clip into the bunched-up figures.

Webster was back, shouting and running as he fired. He came at Archer. Yorgi was shouting too, asking what to do. He wanted to help. Archer covered Webster's run and then his friend slipped and skidded alongside, falling near his boots.

He was up in an instant, shaking his gun hand. "Fuck, think I sprained it."

"Shake it off," Archer growled. "These bastards are serious and crazy as hell."

"Yeah, I got that."

Archer took a second to assess their situation.

"Looks bad. Lots down, but still fifteen or so coming around the car. They're gonna flank us. *Move.*"

Webster ran to the front end. Archer stayed at the back. Together, they opened fire, keeping their enemies at bay. Yorgi shouted that he was moving into the front; a good plan. Archer threw him the keys. Yorgi thrust his body through the gap between the front seats, wriggled around and inserted the key into the ignition. A second later it started, engine revving. The windshield shattered. Yorgi was lying flat along the seats, foot still on the gas pedal.

"Come on!" he cried. "I can drive this bitch!"

Archer loosed two more shots, looked at Webster and gave him the nod. Archer jumped in first, firing through the open back. Webster followed a moment later.

"Go!"

Yorgi jammed his foot down, guiding the base of the steering wheel with the tip of two fingers, still prone. Bullets slammed into the side and now the wheels, but Yorgi wouldn't stop.

The car lurched forward, and Archer saw how close their attackers had gotten as dark figures loomed at the windows and were struck by the front of the car.

"Shit, that was too close," Webster shouted.

Archer had to agree. He found a moment to punch a button and call it in to Cambridge. Before he could finish, the attack again took every ounce of his attention. Bullets came close and men bounced off the car, trying to hang on. There were screams and grunting, fearful shouts that they couldn't be allowed to fail. It was mayhem.

Archer fired blindly through the back window, positive that the enemy would be chasing.

Yorgi's scream of fear came as an utter shock. Archer turned to see another vehicle appearing out of the gloom ahead, coming straight at them. Yorgi didn't have the time nor the position to evade it. The vehicles crashed head on, sending everyone flying forward. They hit hard bulkheads and the backs of seats, but Archer and Webster held on to their weapons.

The car that hit them came to a stop. Through the windshield Archer saw a familiar face.

Greer.

No, what was the idiot doing? Hadn't he seen them?

Greer raised his own Sig and started shooting, right at Yorgi and the British soldiers.

Archer took a bullet in the shoulder, and felt bone break. Webster ducked down, but was forced to kick open the car's rear door and fall out onto the ice-packed road. Three men were instantly upon him, firing without mercy. Archer forced down the horror and grabbed for Yorgi.

"Run," he said. "Just run, mate. Into the ice fields. There's no chance here."

Yorgi's face took on a haunted look, a knowing look, as if the end result of his life had always been obvious.

Archer passed him his backup. "Good luck, mate."

"And you."

Yorgi dove out of the car. Archer fired at Greer, at least trying to take out the traitor before he died. Greer was struck in the chest and then the forehead; dead. A gratifying outcome. But then at least four more figures appeared, lining Archer up in their sights.

End of mission.

Before he died, he saw Yorgi running for the ice fields. He saw the Russian struck by at least two bullets, his body wrenched by the impacts. He saw four men rush over to check on the young Russian's prone body and then walk away with satisfied smiles on their hard faces. It seemed ruthlessly, horrifyingly vicious. Hellishly overstated.

So many men. Almost an army to finish off two soldiers and a civilian. It was a moment of the worst kind of overkill.

Who the hell was chasing down the SPEAR team now?

Archer heard the click of triggers and saw no more.

CHAPTER FOUR

Lauren Fox stood in the air-conditioned cheeriness of her hotel room, happy to be alive. Her second-floor window looked out over Park Lane in London, and the endless colorful stream of vehicles that passed every second of every minute. The red London buses and black taxis went by so frequently that she'd become bored of them, and now drew the drapes.

Smyth looked over from his seat on the couch. "How's that dinner coming?"

She checked the time. "I only ordered ten minutes ago. Give them a chance."

"Hey, it's three thirty. I haven't eaten for four hours. If they don't show up soon I'm gonna be pissed."

"You're always pissed. If I call back and offer to open the door naked, do you think that'd speed them up?"

Smyth shrugged, hiding a smile. "Might do the opposite."

Lauren laughed and looked for something to throw at him, but before she could act, Smyth was up and folding her in his arms. "I'm so glad we agreed to give this a second chance."

Lauren answered by standing on tiptoe and kissing him. Since their last mission, when she'd sneaked away from them in Transylvania to help in DC, she had ended up performing one more time as Nightshade and helped save President Coburn's life. Still, the jaunt had landed her in hospital. She thought the whole experience had helped clarify to both her and Smyth the most important part of this short existence that they lived.

Family. Love. Sharing the things you enjoyed with those you trusted.

A second chance at love? How could she deny that? She'd never stopped loving him.

"This time in London," she said. "I think the entire team needed it."

Smyth nodded. "Yeah, it's been non-stop for so long. We need something different. A change. The other guys are doing well too."

"Well, we were told to take our time. Spend a few days cataloguing the weapons of the gods. A job that could have been done in less than eighteen hours. I guess Hayden realized Team SPEAR had reached their operational limit and needed to recuperate. Kenzie's departure will upset the dynamic." She frowned. "Dahl's more than ready to take some time with his family. Hayden and Kinimaka are trying again. Mai wants to visit Grace in Tokyo. And Drake and Alicia—well, they're in a great place."

"It's all . . . changing," Smyth grunted.

"It's all changed. Finally, everyone is in a good place."

"Speaking of a good place . . ." Smyth nodded at the bedroom door.

"Except for Luther and Molokai," Lauren was saying.

Smyth paused. "What do you mean?"

"Not sure what's happening with those two." Lauren shrugged. "I guess I don't know them well enough."

"They'd better not mess with our mojo," Smyth said with typical irritability. "And Luther better not mess with Mai on their *dinner date*."

"Y'know, I do believe Mai can take care of herself."

Smyth laughed. Lauren checked his pulse. "That's two laughs in a few minutes. What the hell happened to the real you?"

"Dunno. I'm just glad we finished up with those weapons. Cambridge himself locked the vault as we watched and walked away. It's done, so long as the Brits don't mess up."

"Cambridge seems very capable."

"He is. But he has a boss. And that guy has a boss." Smyth shrugged. "Too many cooks, and all that."

"Well," Lauren checked her watch, "it's almost four. I wonder where that pizza is?"

"Probably heard how you might greet them."

Lauren paused, thinking. "Even now, I'm finding it hard to relax," she admitted. "With President Coburn here in the city."

"Yeah, it's like a tick in your eye that you can't get rid of," Smyth said. "Are we on call? Aren't we? The guy starts his speech in thirty minutes, but nobody's put us on alert. Clearly, we're not on anyone's first response list but *are* we on a list?"

Lauren rubbed his shoulders. "I think we're backup, but they can't decide what kind."

Smyth grunted. "I'd call us 'when the shit gets real' backup. Wouldn't you?"

"You can guarantee somebody has our number," Lauren said. "Let's just hope they don't use it."

"They won't," Smyth said with conviction. "The Brits know how to handle this. They got good guys."

"So do we," Lauren said. "But Kovalenko got to Coburn two years ago."

"Shit, don't remind me."

"What time's Coburn dining at the embassy?" Lauren checked.

"Seven," Smyth said. "So we got about three hours to worry. I just wish Coburn wasn't here with his whole family."

"Damn, where the hell's that pizza?"

"Coburn is opening the new embassy," Smyth said. "Whilst Mai and Luther go to dinner. You and I eat Italian—"

"Italian?" Lauren cut in, grinning.

"Yeah, *Italian*. And whilst Hayden and Kinimaka, Drake and Alicia dine together with Dahl, Luther and Molokai. Dahl will be pining alternately for his family and Kenzie, whilst Hay and Kini try to leave early to resume bumping uglies. One thing's for sure—this will be a night of unwinding for us. A good night."

"I like the new Smyth." Lauren snuggled into him. "He's eloquent too."

"And he likes the look of that bedroom." Smyth scooped her up.

"Wait, what about the pizza? If we get busy now I just might end up fulfilling the prophecy."

"Of answering the door naked? No, I'll do that."

"Shit, you'll get us arrested."

"And you won't?"

"With this bod? Not a chance."

Smyth checked the time once more. "It's four fifteen," he said, a bit unsure. "Fifteen minutes before Coburn's speech."

"Are you counting down to something? You're worried?"

"Haven't you felt it lately? The others have mentioned it too. Something hanging over us. Something big. A feeling like something's gonna happen, and we can't control it."

"Others?"

"Drake. Alicia. Dahl. All of them. We felt it before Syria, and soon after. Heard a huge increase in chatter. Uncountable whisperings mostly out of Russia. A huge event is about to go down, and I believe we'll be at the center of it."

"It's tied to Coburn?"

"Not a clue. Nothing's clear. Maybe it's just a consequence of our downtime. Ghosts whispering in our ears. I mean, we're not used to inaction. Maybe having time to think breeds restlessness."

"It does," Lauren said. "Back in New York, my time between clients was the most worrying."

She couldn't help but check the clock. Four-twenty clicked by.

"I think we should wait," she said. "I don't want a distracted soldier. I want a fully invested one."

Smyth reacted as though he'd been crunching the stats in his head. "The speech starts in ten minutes. It's a half hour long. A perfunctory opening ceremony. Then he goes upstairs for dinner that begins at seven with his wife and two children and a few hundred hand-picked guests." He stared at her, looking guilty. "I wonder if the others are thinking the same way?"

"They wouldn't be the soldiers they are if they weren't. Don't worry, Smyth. It's all good. I'm happy we're together, that's all."

There came a hard knock on the door.

"Finally," Smyth grumbled. "I'm so hungry my knees are wobbling."

"Nope, that's your jowls."

"Piss off."

He headed for the door, but at that moment Lauren's cell rang. She tugged it out, worrying now because of Smyth's grim warnings. "Hello?" She pressed the speakerphone button out of habit.

Karin's voice filled the hotel room. She was screaming. *"Get out, get out, get out! Now! They're coming for you. Get out now!"*

Smyth turned to her as everything around them erupted into chaos.

CHAPTER FIVE

The door was smashed in at the same time as the window. Lauren saw Smyth duck and leap for her. Glass shattered. Timbers cracked. The door flew three feet backwards, crashing into a wall. She dipped down as Smyth tackled her about the waist, hitting the floor and rolling toward the couch. She caught a glimpse of dark-clad men pouring through the door at the same time as three more climbed through the window.

All carried guns.

Smyth rolled her past the couch and scrambled behind. Bullets flew, penetrating the material with thuds but missing their bodies for now.

"Stay calm," Smyth said. "We're good."

Everywhere they went, from hotel to safe house to DC apartment, the SPEAR team always stashed weapons in multiple hides. They had been attacked too many times to be complacent.

It was four-thirty. She thought about the coincidence of the timing of Coburn's speech as she reached for the Glock that rested under the couch. Smyth grabbed one for himself. More bullets flew past them, some thudding into the wood frame, others passing right through. A sliver of lead grazed her thigh. She ignored it. The room was noisy, reverberating with gunshots. Both she and Smyth added their own refrains, opening fire. The enemy was so dense they couldn't miss. Several men fell, tripping others behind. Lauren felt Smyth's body touch her own and couldn't help think about how he touched her in a different way, a loving way, and how far away that place was right now.

Damn, we just got back together. How much time did we lose?

She shrugged it off. Smyth had taken care of the men at

the breached window and was crawling past her, flat on the ground. He fired around the couch. A shadow appeared overhead. She didn't look, just fired up, saw a body fly backward. A bullet struck the carpet next to her. Another attacker. She shot him too.

Smyth grabbed her, still firing. "Too many of them. We have to move."

She heard the steel in his voice, the hard edge of controlled ferocity and strength. He changed a mag whilst tripping an attacker, then shot the man as his forehead hit the floor.

"Now!"

He grabbed her arm and rolled again. This time they ended up closer to the breached window.

"Are you sure?" she gasped.

"It's the only way out."

They weren't too far up. They could manage it. Outside, the chance of escape increased. She thought she could hear sirens in the distance, but then the gunfire started again.

Are the sirens for us?

Or, is something else . . .

No time. Smyth turned and fired hard into the mass of their attackers. Lauren counted eight men standing and seven on the floor. They had come well prepared. Lauren and Smyth hadn't had chance to alert the rest of the team, but her phone was in her pocket, and as soon as they got out of here . . .

Smyth dragged her forward. He fired at the closest man, who fell. Lauren then saw men at the back of the room, calm, taking aim.

Oh no.

Smyth opened fire again and again. The mayhem he was causing, helped by her, was extending their lives. Enemies were falling, crawling and reaching over each other. Bullets were fired in all directions. Smyth flung her at the open window.

"Go."

She thrust the Glock down the waistband of her jeans, grabbed the frame with both hands and balanced on the ledge. The drop looked huge and only a small grass verge bordered by concrete lay below. But she couldn't wait. A bullet tore chunks from the wall only an inch away from her right hand. Smyth cried out with adrenalin.

She jumped.

The ground rushed up to meet her, air streaming by. She felt the wrench at leaving Smyth behind almost as much as the impact with the ground. Her legs buckled. Her torso folded. She struck hard, twisting an ankle and banging her knee. Pain shot through every nerve in her body, making her scream. The Glock flew from her jeans, tumbling to a stop three meters away.

She looked up. Smyth was already in the air, falling.

She rolled. He barely missed her. Smyth landed well, still holding his gun. They were a step ahead of their enemies. Smyth pulled her up. Pain lanced through her foot, her ankle, her entire leg. New pain. Horrible pain.

"No, no. Oh God, no. Why now?"

"Is it broken?"

"My ankle," Lauren gritted her teeth, tears in her eyes. "I think so."

Smyth looked past her right shoulder. "Oh fuck, I guess it doesn't matter anyway."

She turned. Men were waiting for them. They were stepping out of a black van on Park Lane, outside their hotel. She could see car drivers slowing, stopping, pulling out their phones.

It was all too late.

"I don't believe this is happening," she said. "Not now."

Smyth stood in front of her. "I'm sorry," he said.

Eight men walked toward them, guns raised, like a firing squad. They discharged their weapons simultaneously.

"Don't be," Lauren said as his body took the bullets a moment before hers. He could have fired back at first. He could even have run. There was an alley directly to their right.

But her leg was broken. She couldn't.

He died with her, together. His arm looped across her body and his eyes met hers just as they faded and lost their light.

Dreams vanished. Lost forever.

She felt the pain, the onrushing blackness. At least they had managed to get this last, beautiful week together.

And then she knew no more.

CHAPTER SIX

Karin Blake was in hell. The call she'd made to Lauren and Smyth might save their lives, but it would end hers. It had been a long, hard week since she'd finished helping Drake with the weapons of the gods.

And even longer since the man with the Russian accent had summoned her, offering her a place at his side as he took down SPEAR and President Coburn.

As he did what his father had failed to do.

Karin had listened to his craziness, his vast, clever and complex plan, and she'd known instantly that it would work. She'd known that SPEAR's, Coburn's, and possibly the first world's only chance was her staying right by his side. She had to be right there when he struck.

It was the only warning they would get.

Karin knelt in the cellar of an old house that sat at the heart of a much older estate. A lord by the name of Hastings owned it, living with a small staff of six that had been ruthlessly murdered. Hastings himself had been trussed up and dumped in the cellar, in case the murderers had need of him in the future.

Karin let the cell phone fall from her fingers, hoping that Smyth and Lauren would get out, angry that Luka had revealed his plan with such short notice. Angry at herself that she hadn't coaxed it out of him earlier.

Luka Kovalenko. The Blood King's son and heir. His own vengeance was underway. Long planned. Meticulously executed. The man was the most terrible of enemies—a crazy genius. Even worse, he'd been raised as the son of Dmitry Kovalenko and had experienced all the horrific delights his father could offer. In many ways then, he was worse than the Blood King. He'd brought an army to the UK, to this estate where he knew he could lie low for a short while.

The swift attack was all President Coburn's fault.

The leader of the free world had bumped up his agenda. Decided to open the new embassy early, a decision which accelerated all of Luka's plans and thwarted Karin's.

It was now 4.35 p.m.

She raised her cell phone, intent on calling Drake. Lord Hastings moaned at her side, trussed up by ropes and in a position that had to hurt after a few hours, let alone three days. Hastings was suffering, but Karin's mission was far more important.

When Luka offered her a place at his side, she'd accepted, but not before she put Dino and Wu on guard, ready to storm in at any moment. Both Dino and Wu had trained with her at Fort Bragg, earning every ounce of sweat until all three of them deserted, searching for a better way of life. They were close, waiting for her call. She'd believed that she could thwart Luka's plans by learning them relatively late and throwing a spanner in the works.

Not this late though. He'd told her this morning and had been close by ever since.

Next, she found Drake's number.

And then, down the stairs to her right, she heard and saw a dozen men and Luka himself coming. They were armed. They jumped off the barrier-less staircase, landing on the cellar floor with guns raised. Karin scrambled from her knees to her feet and looked around for a way out. The cellar was extensive with an open, paved central area surrounded by bookshelves, caskets of wine, shelves full of bottles, boxes and large crates, and more. It ran for hundreds of meters below the house.

It was all she could do to thumb the button that was pre-set to call Dino and Wu. The panic button. After that she grabbed Lord Hastings and made a show of twisting his body around as if checking his bonds.

"Is there another way out?" she whispered in his ear.

"Please . . . please help me."

"I can't help you now, but you can help me," she spoke with regret. "Is there another way out of here?"

Hastings half-turned, regarding her up close. She saw the play of fear, regret and then resolve cross his face. "Past the wine racks, bear right. A small door leads to the kitchen."

"Thank you." She looked away.

Luka approached, flanked by his men and one woman. Weapons were leveled, fingers on triggers. Luka was a tall man, about thirty-five years of age, with short-cropped black hair, a chiseled jaw, and a shark's dead eyes. He had an unnerving quality of being able to stand absolutely stock still when he faced you. He didn't even blink.

He stared at her now.

"Just checking on the lord," she tried, offering a fake smile.

He stared.

"I'm surprised you're still here."

He stared.

"We aren't needed for the initial wave." The woman spoke with a thick accent. "Didn't Luka mention that?" She laughed as if she'd told a hilarious joke.

"There was a lot to take in," Karin said, stalling.

Luka smiled. Karin saw an awful lot of Dmitry Kovalenko in his face. It was unnerving. And when he spoke, his voice grated in the same way the old Blood King's had.

"I offered you a seat at my side. A clear view of SPEAR's beautiful demise. A say in my future plans, including Devil's Island. And you—betray me."

"Like I said, I was checking on Hastings."

"Pass me your phone. If I'm wrong, I will apologize."

Karin knew better. "You've never apologized in your life."

"Well, that's true. So let's say—I won't let Topaz here do everything that she wants to you."

Karin regarded the woman. Apart from Luka, Topaz was the only person she feared among the new Blood King's crew. She stood six-four, with hard muscles and a toned body. She was a killer, a lifelong brawler. A scrub of blond hair covered her skull. Her face and neck were crisscrossed with old scars. Knife scars. Knuckle scars. Every night, Topaz chose one of Luka's mercs and challenged him to a no-rules brawl. Every night she won. Sometimes she killed the man, other times she took the loser to her room. Always, she returned with a smug smile on her face. Topaz was Luka's personal bodyguard, and nobody questioned her.

"I don't mean to upset you, Topaz."

"I would start with your toes," the woman said. "Breaking the smaller fragile bones is an excruciating precursor to the main event. After that I would take your ears and your nose, but I would leave your eyes because I love to see the pain they can reflect. You are military trained, yes? So, you've been taught to withstand pain. I love that."

Karin thought Dino and Wu had about as much time as they were going to get. She glared at Luka.

"You won't succeed with any of this."

"It's already succeeding, Karin. One hundred percent success rate."

She knew exactly what that meant. Smyth and Lauren were down. Drake was next. Then Mai and Luther. Her stomach roiled. Her mouth was dry. She was out of options.

"Topaz," Luka growled. "Take her out. But don't kill her . . . yet. We'll save that pleasure for later."

Karin backed away, edging around the struggling lord. Topaz glided toward her, a grim smile fixed on her face. Rows and rows of shelves filled with bottles of wine stood to her left. If she ran fast enough she just might—

Then Topaz attacked and the ferocity of it was all Karin could think about. Karin had been a civilian with a black-belt until under a year ago, when she'd undergone a rigorous military training course. It had honed her, taught her harsh combat skills, but it hadn't prepared her for this. Topaz was another level. Karin blocked attacks that jarred her bones and caused instant bleeding, black bruises and dead areas. It felt like her entire body was reverberating with pain.

And she hadn't taken a direct blow yet.

Topaz was playing with her. She'd seen this woman take out a mercenary in under five seconds. She'd watched for weak spots. She'd found only one.

Her deference to Luka.

Karin took a big risk and turned to the man now, as if hearing a call. The odd move made Topaz hesitate, and then look at Luka herself. Karin leapt, bringing an elbow smashing down into Topaz's face. The blow staggered the scarred woman, drawing a line of blood. Karin didn't press forward— she knew she would die if she did. She turned and ran.

Pounding down the first aisle, the area was compressed into six feet by shelves. Dusty, and crumbling, they stood to left and right. She worried for Smyth and Lauren, clenching her hands into fists and imagining her call might have come too late. All this prep, all this careful undercover work, and she'd failed. She couldn't even warn the others.

The sound of Topaz chasing her down reinforced that fact. The exit door was to her right, through several rows of shelves. But she couldn't aim for it. Not yet. She needed another distraction first.

Topaz shouted something ineligible. It wouldn't be anything nice. Despite her predicament, Karin felt a small amount of satisfaction knowing she could run just as fast as Topaz.

Then, something nicked her lower calf. She felt a sharp, jabbing pain as she went down, sprawling. Her hands were out in front of her, skimming the floor, grazed by dirt and tiny pebbles. She rolled, shocked to see a small blade sticking out of her leg near the ankle. Topaz was on her in a second.

"No."

"I'm gonna fuck you up now."

Karin twisted, raising both arms in a boxer's defensive movement, catching blow after blow as Topaz leaned in and punched. Once more, her body screamed in pain. She rolled to left and right, felt the blade dig in, and cried out.

She hit the wine shelves with her forehead and grunted. That was the least of her problems.

Topaz knelt at her side, going for the kidneys now. Karin managed to throw her body across the Russian's, suffocating her blows for a short while. In another second they were face to face, nose to nose.

"Don't worry," Topaz breathed. "You won't be joining all your friends yet. He will let you live a bit longer."

"Y'know," Karin said. "He'd like you more if your fucking breath didn't stink so much."

Topaz roared and exploded into action. Karin managed to back away, straight into the wine shelves. With just a brief window of time, she pulled the blade from her calf and threw it at Topaz. As expected, the blonde blocked it with a sneer and came at Karin.

What she didn't expect was the wine bottle swinging around from her blind side. It struck her on the right ear, smashing against her skull. Topaz went down face first, crashing into the ground, grunting in pain.

Karin didn't waste a second. She was up on her feet, flinging the remains of the bottle at Topaz and racing off.

Where the hell were Dino and Wu?

CHAPTER SEVEN

The constricted stairway took Karin into the main house. She slammed the bottom and top doors behind her, saw the key for the top one, and locked it. A narrow corridor ran away, old paintings with old-fashioned frames lining the walls. This was Lord Hasting's private passage to the kitchens. She knew that if she ran in the opposite direction she would reach an alcove close to the front of the house.

Did she have time to use the phone?

Every nerve in her body screamed no, but Karin had to risk it. For all her friends.

Jogging, she plucked the phone from her back pocket. As she glanced at the keypad the door behind her smashed open. Topaz stepped out, gun in hand.

Karin ducked as bullets flew from the barrel. The sound of gunshots in the narrow passage was deafening. One of Hastings' prized paintings was hit; its frame smashing and falling askew, its canvas unraveling to the floor. Karin hugged the wall as much as she was able, narrowing the target, still running.

"I see you," Topaz cried and took careful aim.

Karin's spine itched, expecting the bullet at any second. The passage was straight the entire way. There were no hiding places.

Something reached out from the left. Arms. Strong arms. They caught hold of her arm and shoulder and wrenched her into their embrace. A shot rang out followed by a curse. Topaz had missed.

Karin struggled, striking out. There was a shout and then Dino's voice. "Stop struggling, Blake. I just saved your life."

"About friggin' time." She brushed him off, saw Wu standing alongside and took in their surroundings. They occupied a dissecting passage that curved around toward the front of the house. It too, was lined with paintings.

"Takes us to the main staircase," Wu said. "From there we have a dozen options."

"Great," Karin said. "Let's move."

She could hear Topaz approaching, shouting for backup. They scrambled away, running for the passage. There was only enough room to run single file, and Karin noticed Dino had put himself at the back.

"Gonna get yourself killed with your daft heroics one day, Dino," she panted as she ran.

"Just proving I'm still the best, Blake. You never have and never will be better than me."

"I have a memory that says otherwise."

"Yeah? I hear your memory fails when you get old." Dino laughed.

Karin grinned in the semi-dark, still panting, still running hard. The ribbing over her age was a recent development after she'd accidentally revealed she was three months older than Dino, and six months older than Wu. Of course, the knowledge had delighted them. She wondered how many years they would take to let it go.

"Clear."

She ran out of the passage, stopping at the last moment. It emerged into the downstairs hall, which was spacious and circular. The main doors were to her right, a few hundred feet away. The grand staircase was to her left, its steps about half that distance.

Decision. Out or up?

She listened. There were definite sounds of pursuit, but nothing ahead. The front doors might be too far. The staircase then . . .

The trio veered to the left. Dino and Wu drew their guns. Karin pounded up the plush-carpeted risers. The grim miens of old lords and ladies stared back from the walls, accentuated here and there by a colorful seascape or battle scene. She reached a landing where the stairs curved, and saw two statues balanced on pedestals. She turned.

Dino ran half-facing backwards, gun trained. He was waiting for the first head to emerge from the passage. Karin hoped it would belong to Topaz. She'd known and faced some harsh people in her life—from drug dealers living on her housing estate to deadly megalomaniacs—but Topaz was up there with the worst of them.

And Luka surpassed them all.

These next few days aren't gonna end easy.

Braced for emotional and physical hell, she felt for the phone. At that moment men burst from the passage below, firing. Bullets flew up the staircase, chipping walls and paintings and knocking both statues off their pedestals. Karin hit the floor. Dino and Wu fell back, returning fire.

Seven men exited the passage, giving constant fire. Dino clipped two of them, Wu another. Karin saw Topaz's scrubby head waiting in cover, letting her men be the cannon fodder. If only she had a gun of her own.

"Move!" she cried.

Lying flat, she used her hands and knees to move up the stairs, keeping low. Dino covered Wu before receiving similar protection as both men used their military training to escape the deadly fracas.

But Topaz's men pursued without concern for their own safety. Three spindles shattered under fire as well as an entire section of handrail. Splinters chipped at Karin's clothing and her exposed right cheek. She scrambled onward, reaching another landing.

"Hurry," she said. "I have an idea."

They scuttled in her wake, firing downward. As they reached a carpeted corridor they turned a corner and gained a momentary peace.

"No escape plan, Dino?" Karin asked. "*I'd* have had an escape plan."

"No time for that shit now. We're in trouble here."

He was right. But she knew the house. She'd lived here for

days and had scrutinized the place. They had one small window of chance.

"Where the hell are you going, Blake?" Dino asked. "It's a dead end."

"Dino," she breathed. "This is the moment where you get to prove you're every bit as good as me."

Wu shook his head. "Shit, I don't like the sound of that."

"No," Karin breathed. "The next part's gonna hurt."

It was their fastest route. Their easiest route to avoid being shot. It was Drake's only chance. It was all she could do. Her last effort.

They were all going to die anyway.

If her death helped Drake and the others live . . . it was the least she could do.

Karin sprinted headlong down the corridor. It was lined with doors that looked old but sturdy. By her calculations they would reach its end just as Topaz and her men topped the stairs.

Making their goal tight, but achievable.

"Tuck your arms and head in," she said.

"What? What the fuck—"

She grabbed a heavy plaster bust as she passed, weighed it in her arms, and then launched it at the window ahead. She didn't veer, didn't slow. She leapt in its wake, propelling her body through the air, through the smashed window and out into space thirty feet above ground.

Shards of glass cut at her arms and hips, piercing the flesh, but hopefully she hadn't left any behind for Dino and Wu. As she fell, she continued to pump her legs, trying to stay straight. A surface came up —the top of the huge porch Karin knew was there. Instead of thirty feet, she had fallen ten.

She hit and rolled, felt a stab of pain in her ankles and then her knees. But she didn't try to stop there. A lower porch stood beneath the taller one. She rolled to the edge and leapt again, this time coming down atop the second porch.

She looked up to see an incredible sight.

First Wu, arching his body through mid-air, twenty feet above her. He hit the first porch as Dino launched himself out of the window. A knife flew after him, barely missing the top of his skull. Wu rolled off the top porch, joining her on the second as Dino hit feet first, folded and tumbled to the edge.

"Gun!" Karin cried out.

Wu threw it. He was on his knees, facing the wrong direction, but he threw it back at her with unerring accuracy. The kid was brilliant.

Karin caught it and fired up at the window, deterring anyone from leaning out to take pot shots.

Wu came to her side. Dino took the final leap and joined them. Karin pointed at the edge.

"About eight feet to the ground. Go."

They jumped off the roof of the last porch and landed in a flowerbed. Karin rose immediately, body battered and bruised but never failing.

"Jeez, Blake," Wu said. "You planned that?"

"Well, it was a backup plan but, yeah, I had it in mind."

"You crazy bitch."

"Thanks. That's touching."

Dino stood up last, taking deep breaths. "Me and Wu definitely beat you there. We didn't know what was on the other side of that window."

"Faith," Karin said. "Pure faith."

"Ya got that right."

Karin moved out. "There are some stables across that path. Two minutes out."

Wu looked apprehensive. "Some *what* now? Dude, horses and me don't get along."

"Relax. They've been converted into a garage. There's an old Rolls and a couple of new Fords."

Sprinting, then slowing to allow Dino to train fire on the exposed window, they crossed the lawn in a matter of minutes. Karin cursed as mercs poured out of the front doors, racing toward them. They had less than sixty seconds to get this done. Already, the mercs were raising and aiming their weapons.

"Bollocks. We need more time."

"Go," Dino said, falling to one knee. "I can give you that."

"No!"

She hesitated, reached out. Truth be told, they should be dead already with the odds they faced. But she wouldn't let Dino die in vain.

Wu reached the stable doors and pulled.

Karin stood over Dino to offer a tough last stand. They fired simultaneously, pumping two walls of lead into the oncoming mercs, slowing them down. Topaz could be seen at their rear, taking cover behind one of the white columns that held the porches up. Luka had an army right here, and that didn't include all the fighters he'd positioned in London and Paris.

Together, they stood. She was able to use the gun in one hand and reach around for the cell phone with the other.

Half a minute, that's all I need.

Dino slipped her another mag. She rammed it home whilst juggling the phone, and kept up the barrage.

She heard Wu open the garage doors, two enormous wooden rectangles that grated across gravel as he pulled. The shock of the explosion didn't even register. All she felt was a great whoosh from behind, a superheated wave of fire caressing her body, and the sensation of flying through the air. She lost the gun. Dino was tumbling along with her, all control lost. They hit the ground hard, stunned, turning and spinning, smashing every part of their bodies into the hard earth. Finally, they came to a stop.

Karin lay on her back, staring at a clear night sky. The same stars glittered up there that would be glittering upon Drake, upon Mai and Alicia, if they were still alive. The same stars that had shone upon her a week ago, when life had seemed so good and she'd not had any inkling that it might end so soon.

Wu's body smashed down near her feet. It was scorched, charred and bloody. It was unrecognizable as the man she had known, fought with and loved.

Karin screamed. She felt a movement beside her and felt Dino's hand close over her own. It was all he could do. He squeezed her hard, a final goodbye. Karin called on every ounce of strength, fought the concussion and the pain and finally raised the cell phone to her mouth. The speed dial was already pressed.

"Ey up? This is Drake."

"I'm so sorry. You're all gonna die! The Blood King is coming. The Blood King is coming for you. Save the President. Save yourselves. Run!"

A dark cloud almost overwhelmed her. It rose through her body and her consciousness. Dino's grip was still strong. She couldn't hold on to the phone. It tumbled into the grass. The stars above beckoned.

And then Luka blocked her view.

"She's out," he said. "Now get them both loaded onto the container. Get them ready for Devil's Island."

It was the last thing she heard.

CHAPTER EIGHT

Matt Drake listened to the music of Bon Jovi and raised a half-full Desperados to his lips. It felt good to get out in London and relax. It felt even better to be with his friends,

Well, most of them.

They were convened inside London's Hard Rock Café, an option hinted at by Mano Kinimaka and favored by Drake. The food was good. The drinks were good. The music was—mostly—great. He'd been here an hour now and wasn't entirely sure you could call some of the new tunes they were playing 'rock'.

But as always, it was the company that made the night. Alicia was on good form to his right, teasing almost everyone. Beyond her sat Hayden and Kinimaka. They were close, occasionally whispering. Drake hadn't seen them this emotionally synced in a long time and he felt happy for their second chance. Hayden was feeding Kinimaka's Hard Rock habit by offering to go halves on a couple of new T-shirts whilst keeping an eye on her cell phone. Drake knew they were on call due to the President's local speech, but it was perfunctory. *Everyone* was on call because of the President's speech.

To his left sat Dahl and Molokai. Both had started out looking a little uncomfortable, especially as they were the spare couple, but as the beer flowed and the atmosphere inside the restaurant grew, their inhibitions started to loosen.

Dahl was studying the menu. Drake leaned over. "I don't think they have meatballs, mate."

"Not funny," the Swede said, and turned to Molokai. "Did you think that was funny?"

"He's right," Molokai said, missing the point. "They don't have meatballs."

Drake gave Dahl a thumbs up. The Swede seemed a little stressed tonight, more so than usual. Johanna, his wife, was demanding he return home for a while and Dahl was pushing for it. The only reason he was still here was because of their relationship with Coburn. Just a few more days, then Dahl would head back to DC where he would be able to grab some well-earned R&R. Drake had considered questioning him about his thoughts concerning the departure of Kenzie, but decided those wounds were still a little raw. So far, Drake hadn't missed Kenzie, but he knew during the next battle they fought that would change. He'd miss her animal ferocity.

"You with us?" Alicia leaned in.

"Yeah, just thinking about Kenzie."

"Piss off, Drakey. I never liked that bitch."

"Really? I never noticed."

"She once kissed me in a pub around here, you know."

"Now that, I did know."

Alicia sighed and turned to Kinimaka, pointing out one of the largest burgers on the menu. Hayden shook her head. Kinimaka wondered aloud about the pasta salad. Alicia fell into guffaws as if he'd told the greatest joke of all time.

Drake checked the time. It was 4.25 p.m. The waitress came over and managed to remember their entire order without writing anything down. *How the hell do they do that?* He'd be lost after the first three items.

His thoughts turned to Mai. Despite their split he still loved the Japanese woman and wished all the best for her. In an odd turn of events Mai had agreed to go to dinner with Luther. They would be sitting there now. Luther was the muscled man-mountain Tempest had sent after SPEAR when they'd become disavowed. Luther had hunted them, the only soldier in the world with the strength, ingenuity and pure brass balls to get the job done.

In the end, he started working with them, even bringing his big bad brother—Molokai—along for the ride.

But Mai? And a romantic meal? Drake wondered if she might be trying to take her mind off Grace—the young ward she hadn't seen for so long—but then thought he might be doing Luther a disservice. The guy was cool, if large, oily and a little scary. He should at least give them a chance.

"Now what are you thinking about?" Alicia looked a little cross.

"Mai."

"Are you fucking kidding me?"

"Hey, at least I didn't say Dahl."

"Get your dirty mind off him. He's mine."

They laughed together, both taking another swig at their bottles. Drake noticed the time as he did so: 4.30 p.m. Early for dinner, but they were planning on staying here the whole night.

An odd sensation rippled the length of his spine, as if somebody had walked over his grave. He shivered in the cool atmosphere and turned a curious eye to Alicia. "You feel that?"

Hayden and Kinimaka were also staring. Alicia shuddered. "I think it's infectious. That creeped me out."

Almost in sync the group reached for their phones. The screens were blank. Drake shook it off and leaned across Alicia, so he could whisper to Kinimaka. "So happy for you, pal."

Kinimaka turned, just managing to catch the bottle he knocked over before it smashed to the floor. "Whoops. Thanks, bud. I never lost faith in Hayden."

"Hope it lasts forever."

Drake saw a waitress approaching with their food assembled on a round tray. He waited until all had been served and then dug in. The other great thing about tonight was—they weren't fighting, running, or under duress. They weren't trying to save the world. It was a rare, enjoyable evening.

They ate and listened to the music for a while; watched

the videos on the small screens, enjoyed the escapism. Molokai, who had stripped off most of his robes for tonight, and wore only a single wrapping around his chest, leaned back. Drake could see the lesions and sores across his cheeks. He felt happy that Molokai had begun to feel less conspicuous.

He reached for the pitcher of water and poured six glasses. He lifted one to his lips just as his cell phone rang.

Still holding the glass, he answered. "Ey up? This is Drake."

"I'm so sorry. You're all gonna die! The Blood King is coming. The Blood King is coming for you. Save the President. Save yourselves. Run!"

The barrage of words was so sudden and shocking it caused him to lose his grip on the glass. It fell from his fingers and crashed onto the table with an explosive sound, spilling everywhere. Drake didn't notice.

"Karin?" he yelled. "Karin, can you hear me? *Karin?*"

The others were half on their feet. Dozens of heads swiveled their way. The music boomed but the attention was on Drake.

"What is it?" Hayden asked.

Drake hit the call-back button, trying to reach Karin. But the line was dead. There was no connection.

"Is it Russia? Has something happened with Russia?" Hayden's voice was strained.

The chatter had been building all week, increasing signs that something big was coming and that it emanated from Russia. Every listening agency in the world knew it. The stress surrounding the vague knowledge was enormous.

"No," Drake said, staring at the phone. "She said: 'you're all gonna die. The Blood King is coming. Save the President. Guys, we should get the hell out of here. *Now.*"

"*What?*" Alicia's voice was shocked, disbelieving.

He rose fast enough to knock most of the other glasses onto their sides. Hayden was aware enough to pull out her wallet. Drake was studying the front doors, eyes going wider by the second.

"Holy fuck," he said. "The call came too late."

CHAPTER NINE

Gunmen were at the door.

Drake yelled a warning and then fell back. They'd brought no weapons with them. Hayden and Kinimaka screamed at the restaurant's patrons to get down or move to the back wall. Dahl rose and lifted their table in one movement, giving them something to hide behind. Seeing the flimsiness of the surface he then changed his mind, picked it up with a flex of the shoulders and flung it at the advancing men.

Drake scouted the room as the table landed among the mercs. Two were hit hard and fell. Another got a glancing blow across the head and collapsed sideways. Blood flew. The table skidded into more men, halting their advance. Weapons fell to the floor.

The restaurant filled with terrified screams. Drake saw more men gathering outside the front windows.

The SPEAR team didn't run; they attacked.

In any normal situation, that would be true. But looking at the odds, lacking weapons and being among civilians, put a whole new slant on things. Drake exchanged a glance with Dahl. The Swede nodded toward the bar.

"Really?"

"For cover. Not for using."

Hayden was already heading in that direction. The bar was a long rectangle with hundreds of liquor bottles hanging on the back wall, a wide worktop full of half-empty glasses, coasters and spilled liquid, with several barstools standing in front. Kinimaka arrived first, launching his bulk onto the surface and rolling over. Hayden followed. By now, the fallen attackers were recovering and more were pressing in through the doors.

Drake saw rough, seasoned faces, an assortment of M-4 Carbines, Glocks and HKs, and military gear. They were up against mercs of some kind or another . . .

But how many?

Dozens was the quick answer. He didn't hang around to count. With Karin's terrible warning still ringing in his ears, he ran. Dahl and Molokai kicked two more tables toward the mercs, but it only served to slow them a little, keeping them off balance. Civilians were crawling across the floor, hiding their heads in their arms. Luckily, the mercs weren't interested in them.

Drake leapt and slid off the bar, landing in a crouch on the other side. Alicia was already there, throwing full glass bottles at the mercs. Hayden was at the far end, kicking open the door.

"Hurry!"

Gunfire erupted. Bullets smashed into the bar, ripping huge chunks from it. Drake heard the dreaded thunk as several passed straight through. Bottles smashed along the back of the bar, spilling their contents to the floor. He crab-walked at a fast pace, Dahl at his back, following Alicia toward the far end.

"Who are these goons?" the blonde shouted above the clamor.

"Not a clue," Drake said. "But Karin does."

"We have to warn the others!" It was Dahl's strident voice.

"I know, just give me chance."

The restaurant was in chaos. The sound of gunfire, screaming and shouting filled the night. Drake reached the bar's exit hatch and peered out. The others were racing toward a blind corner, following Kinimaka. Something clicked for him then. Of course, the big Hawaiian had been here before. He'd have explored and would know the layout.

Behind, the bar was still being shredded, the mercs enjoying their work. Dahl was already out and Molokai was a step behind him. Broken glass and mixed liquids covered the floor. The odor was eye-watering.

Drake crunched glass as he moved, straight for the blind corner. As he slipped by, he almost bumped into Alicia.

Hayden was entering a speed dial number. She did it twice before sending them a haunted look.

"I can't get Smyth or Lauren on the phone."

"Dead line?" Kinimaka asked.

"No, it just rings and rings."

Drake gritted his teeth. "Keep moving."

He checked the time. It was 4.50 p.m. They had to escape fast, check on their friends and check on the President. Coburn was due to have made a speech at 4.30 p.m. and then attend a 7 p.m. dinner. There was still time.

More gunfire from behind. Bullets impacted the solid walls standing between the SPEAR team and the mercs. Drake moved off after Alicia and found himself in the café's small merchandising shop.

As Kinimaka already knew, it had a second exit.

They ran through the shop, surrounded by T-shirts, sweatshirts, shelves full of glasses and racks of other merchandise. The small exit door opened onto a narrow road that Drake knew was Old Park Lane. The fresh air hit them as they turned left, away from the front of the restaurant. Drake heard Dahl and Molokai barge through the door at his back.

Head down, he took off after Alicia, fishing his phone from his pocket.

Please answer.

He tried Mai's number, his heart beating faster as it rang. All he wanted was her to pick up, but all he got was an incessant, impersonal ring tone.

"I'll try Luther."

They kept close to the brick wall, hoping the slight bend would shield them from view. The mercs weren't far behind, emerging onto the street. It wouldn't take long . . .

Shouts went up. A couple of bullets were loosed. The mercs started the chase.

Drake almost threw his phone to the ground in frustration. Hayden also tried Mai and Luther, and then

Lauren and Smyth again. There was no mistake. Something was very wrong.

They cut up Brick Street and then Down Street, taking as many dissecting routes as they could, keeping buildings between them and their pursuers. It struck Drake as hauntingly staggering that Karin had mentioned the Blood King's name earlier, because this night, this chase and everything surrounding it reminded him of that horrendous night in DC when they had faced Dmitry Kovalenko.

Another road, Hertford Street, appeared and then they were cutting past Nobu with the towering Hilton to their right. Park Lane was ahead, teeming with all manner of vehicles.

"What next?" Kinimaka cried.

"The President," Hayden said. "We have to contact his security and get over to the embassy right now."

"What about—" Dahl began.

Hayden cut him off. "We don't know where they are. Even if they're fine, they're somewhere unknown. Some restaurant. Some bar. We only have their phone numbers. Maybe we can track them later."

Drake didn't like it, but knew it was the best move.

Alicia gave him a grim stare as they ran. "Mai will be fine."

"She'd bloody better be. And what about the others?"

"It'll work out. They're almost as good at surviving as she is."

"Against so many men?"

"We don't *know* their circumstances. Stop guessing and start fighting. Right now."

Drake saw Kinimaka ahead, step into the flow of traffic and slam his hand onto the hood of a big, bright-white Audi Q7. By the time Drake got there, the Hawaiian and Hayden had evicted the driver and ordered him to get the hell out of there. The mercs were just passing Nobu.

"Where to?" Kinimaka asked as Drake leapt in.

"The American embassy! Move it!"

CHAPTER TEN

Hayden strapped into her seatbelt, waited for everyone to leap aboard, and then slammed the dash. "Drive, Mano, drive!"

She grabbed her cell phone as the car shot forward, swerving to find the lesser used lanes leading to Hyde Park corner. Drake leaned forward, ignoring the road and watching her screen as she called a secure number.

"Agent Jaye," she said, before reeling an identification code off, then a secure password that should patch her through to Coburn's private security detail. They had saved the man's life just over a week ago. Now they were trying to do it again.

"We have credible intel saying there will be an attempt on the President's life," Hayden said when she reached someone. "It's garbled, but it's from a good source. It could be the Russian thing. The Blood King was mentioned."

Without asking for any more proof the listener went away, leaving Hayden with an empty phone line. Both she and the team had proven their worth often enough to be taken at their word. Coburn was even now being hustled off the stage, Drake thought.

Safe.

Unlike Mai and Luther, Smyth and Lauren.

Hayden was already redialing their phones. Kinimaka whipped the car around Hyde Park Corner's huge roundabout and headed down Grosvenor Place.

"Nav says there's roadworks or bad traffic up ahead," Dahl pointed out. "Take Halkin, then Upper Belgrave. We'll work around."

Kinimaka swung the wheel, cutting up a yellow Mazda and heading into Belgravia. The team began to relax as they saw no signs of pursuit and a call came back to say the

President was safe. No threats were imminent.

Dahl sighed. "That's one crisis averted. Now let's deal with the other."

Kinimaka slowed. They knew Mai and Luther were eating in Knightsbridge, which was just a few minutes to the north. They had no clue where Smyth and Lauren might have ended up.

"I'll try again," Hayden said. "But keep driving toward the embassy. Once we're inside I can use their tech to start tracking phones."

"Wouldn't a safe house be quicker?" Molokai asked.

"Maybe, but the embassy's closer and our IDs ensure immediate access."

She threw her phone into the central compartment. "No answer from our friends."

Kinimaka laid a hand on her knee. "They'll be okay."

Drake checked the time. It was 5.20 p.m. An hour ago their world had been a different place. Why did he feel that this was just the start? He turned to Dahl. "What the hell's going on?"

"When I've saved the day, you'll be the first to find out."

"Listen," Hayden said. "I know Karin mentioned the Blood King, but he's dead, right? He died in the battle at Death Valley."

"Oh, he's definitely dead," Drake said. "I remember his death squeal."

"Then, like the Drakester said." Alicia sighed. "What the hell is going on?"

"Could somebody have taken his place?" Dahl suggested. "New kingpins are always on the rise. Maybe they appropriated his name. Used his legend to scare the crap out of people."

Drake nodded. "Sounds plausible. I guess Karin didn't have much time to explain." He didn't need to voice his concern for her, and the regretful memory that her brother and parents had died at the order of the old Blood King.

"I think we should split up," Dahl said. "Hayden and Kinimaka hit the embassy. Molokai and I will station ourselves in Knightsbridge while Drake and Alicia wait for a locale for Smyth and Lauren. We need every advantage we can get."

"That's a great idea," Hayden said as Kinimaka pulled over. "Grab taxis and await our call."

Drake opened the back door. It was 5.30 p.m.

Hayden's phone rang. She held up a finger to stop them and answered. "Jaye here."

A man's voice came through the speakerphone. "We need you. How close are you? We need your help." It was the same Secret Service agent Hayden had spoken to.

"Slow down," Hayden breathed, closing her eyes briefly. "What happened?"

Drake felt his entire body tense up.

"We need you *now*. It . . . it wasn't the President they were after . . ."

Drake wrenched the door closed as the man continued speaking. Kinimaka slammed his foot on the gas.

"*We're coming!*" Hayden cried out. "*Hold the fuck on!*"

CHAPTER ELEVEN

Marie Coburn, the First Lady of the United States of America, stared aghast as two figures entered her bedroom.

"What are you doing?" she asked.

When there was no reply she moved to the nearest window and opened a blind. Light flooded over the scene, bringing a new perspective to the interlopers in the room.

"Is that your dad's shirt? Jeez, c'mon guys. Get a move on. I want to see how you look in your dinner outfits."

Ruby, her youngest at ten years old, flashed a new watch that she'd strapped around her wrist. "It's only half four, mom. Dad just started his speech. Dinner isn't for . . ." she screwed her face up, "a hundred and fifty minutes yet."

"That's right. And I want you to look perfect. Do you think you can do that for me?"

Ruby crinkled her nose. "I can. Not sure about *him*." She nudged her brother and flounced away.

Dean, her oldest at twelve, shook his head with all the world-weariness of an older brother. "I'll make sure she's ready. Don't worry."

Marie smiled at the boy, then stepped forward to hug him. He accepted without struggle, which was a miracle in itself. But then their personal lives had become very *impersonal* during the last three years. Her husband was in his final presidential year and had already announced that he wanted a second term. She didn't mind. She loved playing her part, seeing the good she could do. Yes, many areas of the job were abhorrent, dangerous and just plain annoying—but the good outweighed the bad every day of the week.

She let Dean go and watched him walk out of her hotel bedroom. She had been lying on the bed, catching a twenty minute nap. It was going to be a long night.

She'd laid her dress out on the chaise longue, her

hairstylist was booked for 5.30 p.m. With the dinner starting at seven they were cutting it fine, but Marie was confident—they were long-practiced at this kind of thing. In truth, she was more interested in London.

From her window she could barely see past the high tower block opposite—an office building. From the main room she could see the sweeping bend of the River Thames, the London Eye in the distance past the clump of buildings surrounding Big Ben and most of the way to Buckingham Palace. She'd eaten breakfast that morning whilst taking it all in.

She exited her bedroom, impressed that the children were in their own rooms—hopefully sorting through their dinner clothes. She checked her phone. There were no messages, which was a great sign. Perhaps she could persuade her husband to take an extra day here, a sightseeing day.

Immediately, thoughts of the added security and protocols to work through brought her down. They could never just wander any more. She remembered those times with deep fondness. It was all that she'd wanted. To be free with her husband.

Funny, how fate turned you around.

Ruby stepped out of her room. Marie paused as her breath was taken away. *Oh my, aren't you gonna be a little heartbreaker.*

"How do I look?" Ruby twirled.

"Beautiful, darling. You look so beautiful."

"You think Dad will be pleased?"

"Yes." Marie blinked tears from her eyes. "I really do."

She made a cup of tea and then double-checked with the guards outside that all was going as planned. Ron Seally was her principal guard—one of the older men in the Secret Service detachment—and they'd developed a nice relationship through the years.

"How's it going, Ron? Any proper London paparazzi turned up yet?"

"Unfortunately not, Mrs. Coburn. But if they do I'll be sure to grab one for you."

"Thank you, Ron. I'll look forward to my picture in tomorrow's daily rag."

Seally grinned and turned away. Marie thought he seemed a little distracted, but the Secret Service had a lot on their plate tonight. She should be concentrating on her own chores. She returned to the room and, inevitably, the window.

Tourists wandered the streets below. Vehicles thronged at the traffic lights and then flowed around tight curves. The roads here were tiny compared to those where she'd grown up in Las Vegas, but the footfall looked just as dense.

Ruby called her name. Marie half-turned. She felt a tremendous thud in her chest. It felt as although somebody had pushed her forward with all their strength, but nobody was there. She heard the window crashing a millisecond later, and then realized she was lying flat on the floor.

Unable to move.

There were screams. Shouts. Ruby was the first to see her. Marie didn't understand why she couldn't get up. She managed to raise her right hand only to see it flap back down to the floor.

The hotel room door bust in and Ron was there. Good old dependable Ron. She felt a wetness at her stomach, which was odd. Ron was ducking, crab-walking to her side, shouting orders into his mic and looking stressed.

Marie saw Dean over Ron's shoulder. Her son was crying. And when she looked to Ruby she saw her daughter crying too. *Oh God, why?* And why weren't the Secret Service agents attending to them?

Ron shouted into his mic so loudly Marie heard every shocking word.

"Turquoise is down. I repeat, Turquoise is down! She's been shot in the stomach. Came through the window. Get the goddamn car moving and the hospital prepped. Tell them they have incoming!"

Marie assimilated it all. She'd been shot? Was that why

everything seemed to be moving so slowly? Was she . . . was she dying?

No, not in front of my babies.

Marie fought for life. She saw the blood now, leaking across the floor. Ron rolled her over and pressed a hand against the wound. Other men grabbed what looked like bandages. For the first time Marie felt a stab of pain.

"Turquoise is down," Ron repeated. "We'll use Brimstone. Get a fucking move on!"

Marie knew Turquoise was her own code name and Brimstone was their word for the hospital they'd vetted and partially sealed days ago, just a two-minute drive away.

Ruby was reaching for her, but Marie couldn't respond as Ron lifted her, aided by two other men. They bundled bandages against her stomach. Marie cried out as the pain flared. She saw pools of blood on the floor. Her children were following. She fought to stay awake.

If I'm awake, I'm alive. I will not leave them like this.

They carried her out of the hotel room. Three were in front of her, guns drawn, with two behind. Two more protected her children. They couldn't leave them inside the room. They traversed a corridor and then plummeted seven stories, ran in unison through the lobby and leapt straight into a car that waited outside. Its doors were open. It was heavily guarded.

Marie saw the ceiling and then the sky. She saw flashes of the men protecting her, Ruby and Dean trailing her. She saw Ron and thought his pleasant older face had never looked so grim, so full of fear.

The blooming pain made her groan. It wasn't a bad thing. Pain meant you were still alive. Pain was a genuine, living thing you could grab hold of.

Ron steadied her as they slid into the back seat. "Hold on," he whispered. "Hold on, Marie. We'll get you there. Your children are in the car behind. They'll want to see you. Please just hold on."

Marie Coburn did as she was told.

CHAPTER TWELVE

Hayden's head was reeling. Barely an hour had passed and everything she knew had been turned upside down. When they entered the Hard Rock, her prime concern had been looking after Mano, making sure the big man didn't empty his wallet on souvenirs. She'd been happy. Relaxed. Their relationship was moving ahead in steady increments. For a brief window in time, most of the SPEAR team were content.

Now, their world was chaos. There was a chance London was under attack. She was finding it hard to grasp that the First Lady had been shot. Karin had warned them that the President was in danger, but this was just as close.

And where the hell were their friends?

Those two words—Blood King—sent a deep, creeping chill through her body, as it had ever since he killed most of her team in Miami when they first encountered him, an act that had sent Drake, Ben and Kennedy to her aid. Two of them were now dead by Kovalenko's old Blood Vendetta. Would they ever be free of the madman's memory?

Kinimaka wrenched the wheel hard as they switched lanes, nearing the American embassy. The First Lady was in surgery and the President was insisting on being at her bedside. Team SPEAR had been summoned to help in any way they could. She listened to the others preparing, going through protocols and liaising with teams already on the ground. They would be heading inside the hospital, ostensibly to get first-hand information from the Secret Service and start their own investigation into the incident.

Their warning had been incorrect. Could Karin have gotten it wrong? Had she been fed false information? It would be a whole lot easier to sort if they could get hold of her.

Hayden shrugged it all away and focused on what she

could deal with. The First Lady's prognosis was good. The bullet had missed all the vital organs, but she had lost a lot of blood. Her children were already present at the hospital.

Not good, Hayden thought, but knew the Secret Service always identified and secured these places prior to a visit. Coburn was en route, five minutes out. The SPEAR team wouldn't be far behind.

Hayden concentrated on Kinimaka's driving for just a moment. The Hawaiian was weaving them through the London traffic at high speed, gaining horn blasts and two front passenger side dents, but bringing them closer to their destination with care for pedestrians and no incapacitating crashes.

Her cell phone startled her as it rang and vibrated. It was set to full volume and quivered across the dash where she'd flung it.

"Who's that?" Drake was quick to ask, desperate for information.

Hayden checked the screen. "Unknown caller." Her left fist clenched in the hope it might be one of their friends getting in touch.

"Hello? Jaye here."

"Hayden, is that you?"

"Cambridge? What's happening?"

Cambridge had been their London liaison—the SAS captain that invited them to oversee the placing of the weapons of the gods into the secret vault.

"I'm sorry, but this is about Smyth and Lauren."

Hayden tensed. Cambridge's tone was bleak.

"Oh, please . . ." she said, her voice cracking. Pure dread wouldn't let her stay professional.

"I'm so sorry, guys. Smyth and Lauren are dead. We found their bodies off Park Lane about five minutes ago."

Hayden threw her head back, screwing her eyes tight shut. Kinimaka twisted the steering wheel to the right, pulling into the curb and hitting the brakes hard, unable to trust himself to drive. Hayden heard disbelief and rejection from Alicia and Drake, but their words changed nothing. Dahl punched something hard. Molokai remained silent.

Hayden wiped her eyes. "Just Smyth and Lauren?" She could hardly speak their names.

"Yes."

"Were they . . . together?" Drake asked.

"They were," Cambridge said. "Hand in hand."

Hayden couldn't keep it in. The sobs wracked her body. Kinimaka reached over and enfolded her in his large arms, crying himself. Minutes passed. Eventually, Cambridge asked if they were headed to the hospital.

"Yeah," Alicia answered. "We are."

"I have men there. I'll try to stay in touch."

"Wait." Drake leaned forward, speaking in a husky voice. "Have there been any other reports tonight? Of attacks and deaths?"

"Yeah, I think so. Wait a moment."

Hayden was staring at the roof of the car, eyes closed. Kinimaka was holding her. Drake was almost in the front seat. The others were silent.

"Apart from the Old Park Lane area, which was you guys, we've had one other incident. Two people killed at a restaurant in Knightsbridge about twenty minutes ago. The bodies haven't been identified yet."

Cambridge signed off. Hayden felt empty. Her vision was black around the edges. Outside, cars blasted their horns and people stared. Nothing moved those inside. It was silent in there until Hayden spoke.

"We should head to the hospital."

"Yeah." Kinimaka drew away from her.

"Prepare as best you can," Hayden said. "We don't know if this is over. We don't know if it's all tied together."

"We don't know anything," Alicia hissed. "Let's fucking find out."

"I gotta agree," Molokai said. "We start with the hospital."

"And we don't know where Mai is." Drake clung to hope. "Or Luther. Get moving, Mano, and we'll keep trying."

The Hawaiian restarted the car and blasted away from the curb.

CHAPTER THIRTEEN

Mai Kitano checked her watch. It was 4.30 p.m. She noticed Luther do the same. As one, they grinned.

"Never leave the job alone," Luther said. "Words that keep me alive."

Mai agreed. They were aware that Coburn was giving his speech about now but had turned down their phones, barring the emergency ringtone. The decision to eat dinner early had been made so that their downtime coincided with the others who were spending the night at the Hard Rock.

"Been a long time since I went out on a date," Luther said, then frowned. "And, to be honest, I can't remember the last time I ate in a restaurant."

Mai thought about it. The same was true for her. Drake and she had made the effort a couple of times, and she remembered treating Grace to a night out in Tokyo, but out on a fresh date with a new man—had she ever done that?

"I guess we're both out of practice." She laughed. "And who called this a date? Isn't it a get together for work colleagues?"

"Y'know," Luther shrugged, "I've landed in more war zones than I want to remember. I've been used as bait, as an enforcer, as the tip of the spear. I've been sent on more hunt and kill missions than I can count. But this . . . this place confuses me."

"It's too mundane," Mai agreed. "I keep checking the exits for enemies."

"Ha, me too."

The waiter interrupted their soft laughter by taking their drinks order. It might have been a night off, it might even have been date night, but both stuck to water. Mai yawned, and then placed her hand over her mouth. "Sorry."

"Jet lag? Me too. Every time I fly."

"What makes you think it's jet lag?" Mai widened her eyes.

"Hey girl, you'd better not be yawning at me."

"It takes a lot of man to hold my attention."

Luther tried hard not to laugh, but failed. "And that's something else," he said. "I haven't done this for so long I've forgotten how to do it."

Mai accepted the glass of ice water with a nod. "Me too."

"Shall we talk about work for a while?"

"Yeah, let's start there and slowly improve."

Mai found herself accepting Luther. It was one thing to like someone, another to share a meal. For her though, that would never be enough. She needed to warm to a person, accept them for their flaws as much as their skills. Luther didn't hold back. He was a man that spoke from the heart and laid it all out, good or bad.

"So what's next?" Luther asked.

Mai blinked at him. "I really think you need to clarify that question, my friend."

"I meant with the team. The weapons are safe. Coburn's heading home after tonight. What's next for SPEAR?"

"I guess we go back to DC. Another new HQ, maybe? Then wait for the next mission."

"Is that it?"

"Well no," Mai admitted. "I believe the whole SPEAR operation needs changing. I'd really like to go back to Tokyo for a while. Visit Grace. My sister and Dai. My parents. More than anything, that would give me some peace."

"Cool." Luther watched her, then said, "Want some company?"

"You really want to do all that with me?"

Luther saw her surprise, and looked away. "Maybe," he said. "If you want me. Answer me one important question first."

She couldn't keep the wary look off her face. "What question?"

"Do you still love Matt Drake?"

Mai took a long drink, thinking. It was a great question. "In one way—yes, forever. We moved mountains together. Saved the world. Scorched the earth. We exterminated hundreds of bad guys together, saved each other's lives more times than either of us can remember. He's my greatest love, to be honest."

"And in another way?" Luther would understand all that and have no issues. He'd be the same with any man or woman in his unit.

"In the way you're asking? I regret pushing him away."

Luther nodded. "Of course."

"But . . . I want to move on. I *will* move on. It's just gonna take some time."

Luther nodded again. "That," he said, "is the best and most honest answer I've heard in a long time. I can live with that."

"Oh, really?" Mai shrugged the clinging memories away and rustled up a grin.

"Yeah, really. And it gives you a full backstage pass to all this." He indicated himself from head to toe.

Mai laughed but didn't stop herself from taking a look. It wasn't bad. "The first time I heard of you," she said, "it was savage. You were a legendary warrior, an old school bloodhound."

"As were you," Luther said. "I know about the Coscon stuff, years ago. About Mai-time. You thwarted the Yakuza at least twice and lived! The things you've done—now that's legendary."

Mai sat back as their food came, glancing at her watch. It was 5.05 p.m. She considered checking her phone, but Luther's company and the smell of food had made her more relaxed than she'd felt in months. She didn't want to spoil a potentially great evening. Instead, she ate, noticing for the first time that the front windows of their restaurant overlooked Harrods, London's famous department store.

Crowds streamed past, some running and some lingering; sirens filled the streets; a loud motorbike screamed by.

Just another night in London.

"Is your food okay?" the waiter returned and asked.

Mai had a mouthful of pasta and nodded. Luther swallowed and watched the man retreat. "You think he waited until neither of us could reply?"

"Yeah, it's something they do."

Mai heard raised voices coming from the kitchens and turned a wry smile on Luther. "I guess someone managed to—"

Something caught her attention. Years of surveillance, combat and warfare were engrained deep inside—part of everything she did. Out of the corner of her eye she saw shadows filling the kitchen doorway, and knew they were aggressors.

"Trouble!" she hissed.

It was enough. She knew Luther wouldn't run and hide, and she acted accordingly even before he did. She slipped out of her chair and glided toward them. They couldn't fit more than one man at a time through the door. So far, three were through. They were standing with weapons lowered, as if waiting for orders. They were looking for something.

Or someone.

She gained six steps before they noticed her. Luther was slower, but just as deadly. When Mai's stare met one of the men's, he started in recognition. He yelled a warning, raised his gun. Mai took the fight straight to him, to all of them.

As they reacted she leapt over a table, grabbed a gun, and jerked the barrel up into its owner's nose. Cartilage snapped. She pulled it toward her, knowing he wouldn't let go. She sidestepped, putting him between her and another man. She kicked out viciously, sending him stumbling backward, knocking another opponent into a fourth that was coming through the doorway.

Luther engaged the spare attacker. The huge warrior

looked pissed, no doubt angry at the interruption. His large right hand grabbed his opponent by the throat and shoved him up the wall, legs kicking, until he choked out. A weapon clattered to the floor, which Luther collected.

"Now," he said. "Who's brave enough?"

Mai thought she might have subdued the attack, but a quick glimpse into the kitchen showed more men crowding in, weapons ready. Someone shouted from inside: "Shoot your way through. You have your orders."

Mai stared in shock as gunshots rang out and the man she'd pushed through the kitchen door fell back into the restaurant, blood gouting from several bullet wounds. He collapsed face first. Mai grabbed the arms of the next one to emerge and threw him over the dying man.

Luther came around her, ready with his own gun. "Let me reason with them."

More gunshots sounded from within the kitchen. Luther let loose a volley of his own. A man reeled, taking another with him. In reply, more bullets flew through the door.

Mai glanced around. "We can't risk this. They don't care about collateral, but I do. It's too dangerous."

"Suggestions?"

"We run."

Luther gaped as if he didn't understand the concept. "Now? But we got 'em cornered?"

"No. We don't. They have civilians in there. We have to go."

Luther fired one more volley across the doorway. Mai turned and dashed for the front doors, seeing the endless stream of passersby outside and wondering if she'd made a mistake.

She flung the door open.

Luther paused and fired once more, keeping their enemy a good thirty seconds behind them.

Then they were out on Brompton Road, opposite one of the entrances to the iconic department store. Mai joined the flow of people and sprinted through them, pushing some out of the way. She turned on Lancelot Place and followed it to the right, on Raphael. Luther threw the gun into a trash can as soon as he was sure they were clear.

"We left our phones." Mai stopped for a second, but then kept walking, taking twists and turns that brought her closer to South Carriage Drive and the green vista that was Hyde Park.

"There." Luther spotted a corner shop. "We can grab a couple of prepaids. Who the hell were those guys and how did they know where we were?"

"I'm worried for the others."

They turned right, crossed a road and headed for the shop. The crunching of tires brought Mai's head around and she turned to see a black transit van pulling up to the curb. Before she could shout a warning, the side doors were flung open and men poured out.

Luther whirled. A grim smile curled his lips. "I do enjoy a good brawl."

Steps away, they couldn't stop him wading into them. Luther was a giant, over six-foot-six of solid muscle with the best military training and experience.

Mai saw Kevlar-clad bodies smashed to their knees, tumbling to left and right, hurled back against the side of the van. Metal buckled. She leapt into the fray to help him. She saw a knife flash, blocked the blade, and snapped the arm that wielded it. She whirled and pivoted, sent two men into oblivion with hard punches.

A fist connected with her spine, another with her kidneys. She sent elbows backward, caught at least one of the cowards. She bounced off Luther's shoulder, and spun around. He kicked one man so hard he folded and never came back up. He caught another around the throat and choked him out whilst dealing with one more.

Mai saw more knives flashing. It was all she could do to block them, to disarm their owners. A raised handgun caught her eye to the right and she pounced at the man that held it, punching his eyes, throat and nose until he slithered away. They were both in amongst it now, surrounded by their enemy. They stumbled over the fallen. They could see the interior of the van, dark and stinking and stained with blood.

They were not the first abductees.

A blow at the back of her neck staggered her. Another came in from the left, almost breaking her jaw. Mai saw stars. She'd fought her way out of a crowd before, but this was harder. They were being pulled down. Overwhelmed by the sheer force of bodies, indifferent to the fate of their colleagues. It felt like every man for himself even though she and Luther were the enemy. She caught a wrist and twisted, but for every wound she inflicted she was taking one in return.

Luther heaved and used elbows and knees. Men fell away with misshapen faces, fractured skulls and broken necks, but even he was flagging.

Another van turned up, disgorging more men.

Mai saw more knives raised around her. She was tired, bruised and wondering who might have sent this crazy horde against them. She was worried for Drake and the others.

"Stop!" a voice commanded. "Move aside."

Mai half-crouched, ready to pounce. Luther pushed men away to create space. Emerging from the midst of the new arrivals was a tall, thin man twirling a baseball bat. Mai thought the odds could hardly get any worse and decided to take a few moment's break.

"What do you want?"

"The famous Mai Kitano." The tall man eyed his fallen and broken men. "As impressive as your reputation suggests. And Luther too, the blood warrior. It's good to see you fight, it will be even better on Devil's Island."

"What's Devil's Island?" Luther asked.

"You'll find out very soon after we drop you off there. In all your days you have never seen anything like it."

"How about telling us what's going on?" Mai asked, breathing deeply, prepared to act. "Who's paying for all this? Just for us?"

"Just for you?" the thin man laughed. "You're good, Kitano, but not that good. This is about everyone you know and love. This is about President Coburn, and his family. This is about . . . blood vengeance, courtesy of the Blood King."

Mai showed no reaction. Luther was ready, she could tell. Their attackers seemed to have relaxed a little due to overwhelming numbers. Mai counted fifteen standing, with eight on the floor. Some of those standing were wounded.

"That's a nice bat you got there," Luther said. "Do you play baseball?"

"Not in the conventional sense." The tall man slammed the head of the bat into his left hand. "If you know what I mean."

"Oh, I do," Luther answered, and then to Mai he said. "You ready?"

"Very."

They burst into action. Mai grabbed a shorter merc standing three feet from her right hip, spun him as much as she was able, and plucked the handgun from *his* right hip. She raised and fired it.

Luther was engaged in a similar move. The noise of their gunshots resounded around the neighborhood. Two men fell, wounded and then two more. Mai and Luther were running.

"Shop," Luther growled.

"I know," Mai gritted back.

They banged through the doors, exposed for just a few seconds and hoping they were more valuable to the thin man and his bosses alive than dead. Inside, the shop was dim and air-conditioned. Shelves were high and densely stocked.

Luther ran down the first aisle, spotted a revolving rack full of mobile phones, and grabbed the cheap ones. Without stopping to pay he ran straight past the counter and into the back. Mai followed. A female teller screamed; and then an older man stood back as they raced past. He did not try to stop them.

"If we're followed, don't resist," Mai yelled back at him. "Stay safe."

Exiting through the back, they traversed a number of streets, getting lost once more. This time, though, they climbed a wall into a sleepy mews and merged with a thick stand of trees. Inside, it was silent. Standing, staring at each other, they breathed heavily and wiped the sweat from their faces.

"Not what I imagined from a first date," Luther admitted.

"Oh, I've had worse." Mai ripped open the packaging of one of the phones. It was 5.40 p.m. Quickly, she entered Drake's number and pressed the call button.

"I hope everyone's okay," she said in a quiet voice.

CHAPTER FOURTEEN

Drake, seated in the back of the car, raised his cell phone when it rang. The screen read: *Unknown Caller.*

What now?

"Who is this?"

"It's Mai and Luther. Are you all okay?"

Pure joy swept through him. "Oh, shit, yeah we're all good. We weren't sure you'd survived. They said two died in a Knightsbridge shooting."

"Oh, no. Two died back there?" Drake heard her pass the news along to Luther.

"It's worse than that," he said before she could go on. He paused, unsure how to continue. There was no right way to express bad news, no perfect words. There was no easing into it.

"Smyth and Lauren," he said. "They've been killed."

Mai was silent for some time. Kinimaka threaded the car through traffic as the hospital loomed ahead.

"I'm truly devastated," the Japanese woman said. "I can't say."

"I know," Drake replied. "Everyone else is fine, although we all came under attack. We don't know what's going on yet. The First Lady has been shot. We thought Coburn himself was the target, but it appears not. She's in surgery, expected to be okay. The President is at her side. We're approaching the hospital as we speak."

"Should we come to you?"

"Probably, but contact Cambridge first. He's our go-between. Talk to him and see if anything else has come up."

"Understood."

"Thank you, Mai." Drake made ready as Kinimaka pulled up to the curb before a wedge of police. "You and Luther—be careful, and I'm sorry you had to hear about Smyth and Lauren this way."

"It's okay." Mai sounded as downhearted as he felt. "I'll be in touch soon."

Kinimaka opened the front door. Alicia took a moment to place a hand on Drake's knee. "It's okay to show the grief," she said. "Even now. Even here. We all feel it."

Drake squeezed her hand. "Thanks," he said. "But here . . . we're soldiers."

Outside, Kinimaka and Hayden were displaying credentials and gaining clearance. Beyond the police cordon was a Secret Service barrier, which took long minutes to pass. Kinimaka left the keys to the Audi behind. Drake checked the time.

5.40 p.m.

He'd imagined hours had passed since this nightmare began. His heart was shredded, alternately happy to find out Mai was alive and then devastated when he thought about Smyth and Lauren.

Inside, as out, the hospital was heavily guarded. They were checked again and again. In the end, as they passed an empty room on the third floor, Hayden ushered them inside.

"It's taking too long," she said. "We have to take care of this now." She regarded them all with a grim face. "I hate to say this—but call your loved ones."

It was what they'd done during the old Blood King's reign of terror. Now, Kinimaka called Kono, who was back in DC. His sister answered and promised to listen to the FBI guard they were sending over. Dahl's wife accepted the protection too, but not without expressing annoyance. As a courtesy, Drake called Dai Hibiki, so that Chika, Grace and he could prepare for all eventualities. Soon, they were ready to move again.

"I'm praying it doesn't reach our friends and families," Hayden said.

"It already has," Drake said. "Right into this room."

"At least Coburn is unscathed, and the First Lady will be okay. This hospital is impregnable now and well . . . we're here," Molokai said.

Along the third floor, their presence and reputation preceded them. Nods were acknowledged, and more than one respectful set of eyes stared as they walked past. The hospital was quiet, the walls bland and clean, the floor polished. Nurses looked up from their stations as they passed. Open doors revealed patients sitting up in bed, watching television or staring into space. Announcements blared through speakers positioned overhead.

"How far?" Dahl asked.

"Part of the eastern wing has been sealed off," Hayden said. "It's just up ahead."

"At least we helped save the day," Kinimaka said. "It would have been worse if the President or his wife were killed."

"Yeah, we thwarted something," Molokai said. "Don't know exactly what."

Drake felt a small sense of pride that his team had possibly helped prevent an attack. Of course, nothing was clear but the way some of the agents they passed nodded and smiled, it was obvious they had heard more than one SPEAR story.

Hayden pointed out a small sign. "East wing ahead."

The corridor remained the same, with rooms to either side and the occasional nurse's station. Drake expected to see a procession of guards, but they came across only two. Both carried radios. Hayden and her colleagues were expected and waved on through.

They came to a door they were told led to a suite of rooms. Hayden pushed through into a large waiting room, walked all the way across, and then entered a wide corridor. A door stood open ahead and to the right, bright light spilled from the room.

It was eerily quiet.

"After everything we've been through to get here," Alicia said. "This feels weird."

Drake agreed. But as they came closer all that changed. A

man's low groan reached their ears, followed by a child's sobbing. Drake and Dahl reacted, springing ahead. They reached the open door and looked inside.

Agents were everywhere: bleeding, dying, crawling through each other's blood. The First Lady had collapsed onto the floor, clutching her wound. Both of Coburn's children were huddled into a corner, guarded by a solitary, wounded man.

There was no sign of the President.

"My God," Hayden said. "What happened here?"

The First Lady looked up, eyes wracked with pain. "Hayden, is that you? Oh, thank God. They took him, they attacked us and took him. Warned us that if we raised the alarm in under ten minutes they would . . . they would—" her eyes darted over to her children "—hurt him."

"They took the President?" Kinimaka questioned. "Who? How? When?"

Hayden was already inside the room, heading for the First Lady. Molokai and Dahl checked the unmoving men for signs of life. Drake and Alicia ran to the wounded. Drake recognized some of the dead Secret Service agents as many of the President's closest guards.

Hayden steadied the First Lady. "Tell us what happened. Did they say anything?"

"They took great pleasure in telling me. At least, one man did. He was called Luka. He also said he was the Blood King. The Blood King's legacy, I think. I don't know. They prepped the hospital for months, knowing that eventually the President would come to London to open the new embassy. It was a guaranteed scenario, he said. They were ready months before we came. Months." The First Lady started crying and then coughing. Hayden helped her sit up and propped her back against the bed.

"They used insiders; men and women whose families were threatened. They knew which hospital I'd be taken to if I was wounded, or in care. *They knew.*"

"You were shot so that Coburn would come here?" Alicia asked in shock. "Are you kidding me?"

"I led my husband here." The First Lady wept. "And they were ready for him."

Drake checked on the children and the older Secret Service agent guarding them. "We have to get some medical attention in here," he said. "Where did they go?"

"Out." The First Lady pointed at the door. "Out and then right. Ron watched them, and then came back for the kids."

"Escape route is through the east wing," Hayden said. "And then—something elaborate. If we can't catch up now—he's gone."

"Then move," the First Lady told them. "Please . . . save my husband."

The SPEAR team gathered up what weapons they could find and moved out.

CHAPTER FIFTEEN

Drake raced away from the First Lady, the dead men in her room, and her crying children, followed by the rest of the SPEAR team. The security guard, Ron, scrambled for a communications system, since all theirs had been knocked out when they were attacked.

Drake turned right out of the room and dashed along a corridor lined with windows.

Who the hell is this Luka? How can he call himself the Blood King?

Despite the questions plaguing his brain, Drake came to a junction and stopped. He held a hand up. They listened. It was deathly quiet down this end of the corridor and there was no movement either way. He checked again.

"We should be—" Alicia began, but Drake held up a hand. They were just minutes behind their quarry.

A scrape. A muffled voice. Echoing from the right. The team ran, checking the weapons they'd collected from the dead and wounded agents. It was a scrappy selection for their tastes but the best they could do for now. The corridor was dim, illuminated irregularly. They came to another junction, ran to the left.

"It's a bloody warren," Dahl said.

"It's an old hospital," Hayden said. They passed numerous services stairs and elevators they were forced to check before continuing. "But I think we're catching up."

Drake agreed. Still, they needed to be cautious. Their prey could have left snipers behind.

"Luka? The Blood King? A legacy? What the hell's going on?" Alicia asked.

"We'll find out," Dahl grunted. "When we get Coburn back."

Kinimaka had snagged a radio back in the room and now

brought it up to his mouth, ready to call in backup. Dahl stopped him with a hand on his forearm.

"They could be listening. All we have is the element of surprise."

Kinimaka nodded. Drake ran faster, gun out, prepared for the appearance of an enemy, always aware of his escape routes. Out of the corner of his mouth, he whispered, "Try Karin again. She's the only one that might know something."

The task fell to Kinimaka, who was situated near the back of the pack. Molokai watched their rear. The Hawaiian pulled out his phone and tried her twice but the line never picked up.

"No answer," he said. "It doesn't mean . . ." He clammed up.

They all knew what it might mean. Dahl came up with the idea of contacting Kenzie. Before anyone could answer he fell back and made the call. Drake saw the Swede's face—creased with worry and tension.

"No answer," Dahl said. "This is not good."

"You know Kenzie," Alicia grunted. "Could be anywhere from a thousand feet down, digging up a pharaoh, to a few thousand feet up, earning her mile-high badge."

Dahl ran with her. "Is that supposed to make me feel better?"

"It's the truth, Torsty, and you know it."

Ahead, Drake caught a glimpse of something—a figure maybe. It was a flash and then it was gone. He slowed, signaling the others. They switched to dashing short distances, from one empty room to another, in pairs. They used both sides of the corridor.

They heard hushed voices. Guttural tones. Drake couldn't pick anything clear out of it—just disjointed echoes. As they traversed a short corridor, the team waited until another junction appeared, and then ran again. At the corner they halted and peered around.

Ahead, in the semi-dark, they picked out at least twelve

men, all wearing some kind of chunky body armor. At first, Drake couldn't see the President, but then thought he saw a figure near the front, being dragged along.

"It's a fucked-up situation," Dahl said. "The corridor. Their numbers. Firepower. Their hostage. We can't win."

"Stay quiet," Drake said. "The next part of their plan might—"

His phone vibrated. He fell back and motioned to the others, conscious that it could be Karin, or even Kenzie, calling back.

Drake answered without checking the screen. "Yeah, who is this?"

"Cambridge again."

Drake expected the SAS captain to quiz him, to be aware of their situation and ask for a position. Instead, the man shocked him.

"I have some really bad news, Drake."

His heart hit his throat. Alicia, watching him, frowned deeply. Drake managed to find his voice. "What bad news?" He was thinking of Karin, of Kenzie. Even of Mai and Luther.

Everyone whipped their heads around.

"Yorgi," Cambridge said. "I received a distress call from the men I assigned to him. My men found their bodies, Drake, along with Yorgi's. I'm very sorry."

Drake was crouching with his back against a wall. He slipped down it, landing hard, feeling the breath ripped out of his body. The world went away and all he saw was spinning black spots. From somewhere distant he heard people hissing his name, felt them tapping his arms and shoulders. He owed it to them to respond.

Briefly, he told them.

Drake fought for air, for lucidity. He would never be the same. But he was a soldier, and circumstances dictated that he should file this news alongside the news of Lauren and Smyth and get on with it.

President Coburn was being kidnapped.

This wasn't unlike Dmitry's Kovalenko's old attack on the SPEAR team. Drake imagined this new Blood King—if that's what he was—had been planning this for many months and was using overwhelming force. The thought helped him sit up and focus. It helped him compartmentalize. He fixed his eyes on Alicia's face and climbed to his feet.

Dahl wiped his own eyes. "We're gonna rush these bastards."

"Wait," Hayden said in a harsh voice. "We can't risk the President."

"If they get him out of here," Alicia said, "he's dead anyway."

Drake looked ahead. It felt as although he'd been sitting on the floor for an eternity but, judging by the position of their enemy, it could only have been seconds. He stared at the phone still clasped in his right hand.

"Cambridge," he said. "Get a fix on this position. We're staring at the President who's being dragged away by at least twelve men. We're gonna try to rescue him."

"What? That might not—"

Drake didn't argue, just ended the call and pocketed the phone. He figured their enemy was thirty feet away, coming up on another junction. They were nearing the extremes of the hospital and had navigated to the rear. It wouldn't be much longer before their escape plan took shape.

"Move," he said.

They ran fast up the now empty corridor. Drake saw Coburn being dragged along, the tall man protesting. One important thing he knew about Coburn was that the man was ex-military. The man was a fighter.

Drake reached the end of the corridor and raised his gun.

CHAPTER SIXTEEN

Luka Kovalenko helped drag President Coburn along, at the head of his men, the highly efficient Topaz at his side. This had been a long time coming. It had been part of his wider plan since his father was killed.

Back then, his world had degenerated into a living hell. His father had ruled the criminal world with such a violent fist, with such severity and hard-heartedness that, upon his death, the sharks had circled. Kovalenko's empire crumbled. His men deserted. His lieutenants walked away. All of this instant abandonment was down to the Blood King's way of ruling—by coercing his men, by threatening their families, by killing a man a day for as long as he sailed on that huge fucking boat.

Luka had been thirty-three when his father died. In the Russian gangster hierarchy, that made him little more than a child. In the past, he'd run some operations, killed some men, but nobody pointed out the mistakes he made. Nobody had helped him improve. Nobody wanted to draw his father's attention. Luka had always been a step ahead of them with his intelligence though. He knew how everything worked.

As the years passed, he grew accustomed to privilege. To being waited on prior to and after the odd dirty job that his father threw him. He enjoyed the wealth. He looked forward to being summoned to the boat, where his father would impart a lifetime's knowledge in just a few days, where he would be asked to choose and then kill that day's human sacrifice.

Life was good for Luka until the day his father died. He even met a woman that he loved, a soul that he cherished, until Dmitry found out and had her removed. Luka never found out what happened to Darla, not all those years ago and not in the time since. It didn't help that everyone close to the old Blood King had either died or disappeared.

Luka knew the blades were being sharpened as soon as word reached him of his father's death. He knew the circumstances. He'd been privy to every nuance of his father's plan. The shock of the great man's murder rocked Luka from his head to his toes. Dmitry had seemed invincible, the great castle that could never be breached. Luka had imagined living in his father's shadow until he himself was an old man.

Life threw him the biggest challenge right then. Luka knew Dmitry's empire would shatter. Nobody could hope to shore it up, not even Luka. Those oppressed soldiers and lieutenants would scatter, along with the ones tasked to watch their families. It was the greatest and only opportunity they were ever going to get, and in truth, Luka couldn't blame them.

But it did leave him wallowing in the blackest of black holes.

Luka vanished. The men—and there were many—that came to kill him found only empty rooms in an empty house. They didn't know Luka was alive, struggling along with the cesspool of humanity. He cut his hair and took to wearing glasses. He grew a beard. He lived sparsely, using money he'd secreted away after various jobs. His father had cautioned him to do it. His father had always known that bad things sometimes happened.

The Blood King being the worst of them.

It hadn't occurred to Luka to fade away. He was his father's son and wouldn't let the memory of the man be lost. Nor his legacy. Luka vowed to find a way to rebuild the empire.

He started by employing the best of the best—Topaz.

Luka didn't have the time, nor the reach or skills, to force people to join him back then. He'd lived in a one-room squat overlooking a meat factory and a railway line. Twice, during dreadful nights, the stench emanating from the meat factory had made him throw up. The trains were endless, their incessant rumbling setting his window and single cupboard jangling, plaster wafting from the ceiling and the old drunk next door cursing at the top of his voice.

After the third night the old drunk didn't curse any more. Luka used his apartment to store acquisitions he didn't want in his own. Three times, during this period, Luka came close to the men that wanted him dead. Twice, he dealt with men on the street tasked with the mission of finding Luka Kovalenko. He didn't falter. His back story was solid, his false papers and documents perfect in every way. He even ended up recruiting those two men into a satellite business of his own.

The third would-be assassin proved harder to shake, appearing outside his squalid apartment on a biting cold December day. Luka remembered this man—he'd been one of his father's shrewdest enforcers and Luka's teacher on several occasions. Luka worried that he'd be recognized. Topaz was out of town, attending to a new business acquisition. Luka was no match for the enforcer alone.

But that, he'd thought back then, *was before I lost it all.*

With a few rubles he used a couple of down-and-outs to lure the enforcer to an abandoned warehouse. There, amid the old crates, the free-running rats and stench of decay, he'd faced the man, holding only two knives.

"Andrei," he said. "You're going to kill me now?"

"Your father was a great man but an even greater monster, Luka. I take no pleasure in this."

"Put the gun away."

Andrei regarded him. "You think you can best me with the knives? Take the easy way out, my old friend. A bullet will be quicker."

Luka kicked rubbish across the floor. "You were one of the best," he said. "Clever. Fast. Brutal. You never questioned my father. I want men like you, Andrei."

"What does that mean?"

"I am rebuilding the empire."

Andrei blinked in shock. It would have been a fine moment to attack, but Luka refrained. Across the entire world, in his whole life, he would encounter just a handful of men and women that could enhance his life. Andrei was one of them.

"The Blood King?" Andrei asked in disbelief. "I am sorry, but your father was one of a kind."

"I don't want to be *the* Blood King. I want the legacy."

"But Luka . . . I can't tell you how hard that will be."

"I want the challenge. I am my father's son, but I have learned from his mistakes. I will start by paying a wage a man can't turn down rather than threatening him."

"And where will you get that kind of money? Your father's accounts were drained; or first frozen and then drained by the Americans. He might have had one or two they don't know about . . ."

Luka stopped him. "I don't care," he said. "When I said I want the legacy I meant *all* of it. From the ground up. From here—" he indicated the squalor that surrounded them "—to total control. To ships, mansions and cars of gold. To life or death over anyone, everyone. To owning governments . . . countries. I can take it all back, my friend, with the right help."

"Like I said," Andrei grunted. "How?"

"Because I know how *he* did it. I remember every lesson that he taught me. I will start by amassing hundreds of small yet significant businesses quietly, anonymously, which I will then unite at a later date under one banner. My advantage is my intimate, insider knowledge of all these businesses. I know who to target, who to break, who to bend and who to bribe. I already know all this, and so do you."

"Listen." Andrei appeared to have stopped listening. "I am employed by one of your father's worst enemies. Dita Nine Fingers. I'm sure you remember him."

"I remember the finger." Luka winced. "The one my father removed."

"Yes, and then Dmitry coined the new name so Dita could never forget. This is real retribution. It will never end."

"I could move Dita further up my to-do list," Luka suggested.

"What? Kill Dita? I'm sorry, but you are going to have to show me more than words," Andrei said. "I am going to have to see action."

With that, the two men clashed. Andrei dropped the gun, unholstering a curved machete that gleamed in the low light filtering through broken, filthy windows. Luka matched the deft man's blows, sharing sweat with his one-time mentor, deflecting and then attacking, forcing Andrei back. It was a studied battle, a demonstration almost, as Luka showed Andrei that he could fight back.

Finally, Andrei wiped his brow and threw the machete, blade first, at the floor. It shuddered as it stuck in, glinting. Andrei threw his arms wide. "What do you want from me?"

Luka grinned. His empire was starting to take shape.

They started small and nameless. A shadow. They took over the reins of hundreds of profitable, well-placed businesses. Luka used Topaz for the muscle, and then others she brought on board, offering pay-checks that, at first, almost broke the bank. But with more persuaders came more money, and better profits. It was the same at the business end. Luka employed astute workers, people shrewder than himself. And he reaped the profits.

Finally, he moved out of the terrible apartment, but he never sold it. Occasionally, he returned to remind himself of how far he'd fallen, and what he'd risen from.

But he was still no Blood King.

Luka built and built, taking almost two years to get to where he was now. The people were in place, the plan was honed. He was ready to announce himself as the new Blood King, to start taking back everything he wanted, but first—

First there was the matter of revenge.

Pulling the President of the United States along the

hospital corridor against his will was satisfying, but the new Blood King had a hundred more delights planned.

Topaz touched his arm. "They have caught up to us."

Luka cursed and pulled Coburn harder. "Do you know who it is?"

"We can't tell yet. They haven't engaged."

"Let me know as soon as you do. And if Coburn gets any slower give him an ass-kicking for me."

Topaz flashed a particular smile that Luka knew she'd never share with anyone else. It was just for him. Topaz's face was still bruised from last night's merc-bashing, which had lasted an entire minute rather than the usual two. This time she had elected to sleep with the beaten man rather than kill him. By morning, Luka saw with mirth, the man was as good as dead anyway.

They were almost clear.

Ordering men to scout their rear and others to check ahead, Topaz obeyed him by kicking Coburn's ass. The President sped up but complained about a knee injury. Luka knew the man was ex-military. He'd read nothing about any injury.

"Run," he hissed, "or I make you run. With fewer fingers."

Coburn appeared to try harder. Luka accepted it for now. They were well protected here. He was being updated through the communications device in his left ear. He had men outside, inside, and all around London and Paris. Other men in other countries. The network was sprawling—worldwide.

They'd taken out Yorgi, Lauren and Smyth. Luka grinned at that. Unfortunately—so far—they'd missed Mai and Luther. They'd also failed to kill the rest of Team SPEAR, but Luka had expected that. More opportunities were planned.

But first, he had to get Coburn out of London.

"Do you know?" he whispered in Coburn's ear as they moved. "Do you know what I'm going to do to you once I get you out of here?"

"You will fail. They'll catch you and then—I will be the one in charge."

"I've prepared everything. From a high-rolling, lush suite in Paris, I'm going to auction you off on the Dark Web." Luka laughed as he grabbed the man's wrist and wrenched it hard. "How does that sound?"

"You won't get away with this. Whoever you are."

Luka knew the President was baiting him. At this point the mysterious kidnapper is supposed to reveal his identity and the entire plan. Luka wasn't ready to do that yet. The revelation that he was the son of Dmitry Kovalenko and the new Blood King would come right after the President sold at a terrorist auction.

His plans were coming to fruition.

Topaz looked over, sending a hooded warning smile. He grinned back, tolerating it. On the one hand she could be overbearing, jealous and crowding, but on the other she was pure gold sent straight from the hottest furnace of Hell. The best fighter, the best bodyguard, the fastest human he'd ever seen, she added layers of threat and protection to his persona that no one in the world could. And he knew that she loved him. She'd betrayed herself a dozen times. He played on that, worked it, used it. The upsides far outweighed the down. With her and Andrei watching his back, Luka felt almost as invincible as he once believed his father to be.

I will resurrect the Blood King's name through any horror. This to honor my father's name and live up to my own legacy. This to preserve a legacy of my own. This to win where my father did not.

The hospital idea had been worked and reworked long before they knew the date of Coburn's visit. When the old American embassy in Grosvenor Square was sold and another building found, Luka's intelligence people knew the US President would come to London to open the new one. Preparation began that very day. Numerous plans were honed, but the news that Coburn's family would join him put the icing on the cake for Luka. He got to order the shooting of the First Lady too. The hospital was long-since prepped—men and women bought or threatened, some killed and replaced by Luka's employees. His eyes were everywhere.

Paris was the culmination although. And only hours away. Luka liked tight deadlines.

For a moment he thought beyond Paris, to three more major plans already in place. He thought about his side venture—Devil's Island. Both Karin Blake and her partner—Dino—were inside a container waiting to be shipped to the island.

Two more would soon be joining them en route to the home of the Devil himself.

It didn't matter which two. Luka would be happy with any members of the SPEAR team. He'd originally planned for a total of three, but four would do just fine. The future was everything he'd ever dreamed it could be.

From the dreadful night of his father's death, escaping torture and murder, he had come this far. Yes, he'd made mistakes—recruiting Karin to help fight against SPEAR had been one of them—but Luka had rebuilt a terrible kingdom. It was now just a matter of bringing it all together. Coburn would cement that, and warn off the underworld sharks once and for all.

"We're approaching the café," one of his men jumped on the comms.

"Good. Then it's all the way down."

"Drake. Hayden Jaye, Torsten Dahl. They've all been spotted behind us."

Luka grimaced. All this work, all these years of effort, and now everything happened at once. He wasn't ready for the key players yet. He didn't want them this close. But they were too capable, too pre-emptive to be allowed to follow.

"Keep them pinned down. We need time to get this bastard out of London."

CHAPTER SEVENTEEN

Kenzie sat in a plush armchair, at the center of a high-ceilinged, dilapidated warehouse. She crossed her legs. To left and right, and behind, rows of crates, boxes and packages stood beside and atop each other, all open, all inventoried. In front, a line mostly made up of men, waited in turn for their names to be called out.

Kenzie counted them again. Eighteen to go, with eight already interviewed. There was still a chance she would find somebody worthy today, but it was worrying, since yesterday's line of hopefuls had proven inadequate.

She sat back, moving her legs slightly as the latest candidate approached.

"Hey, name's Pearce. Forty-one with experience. Dependable. Fast. Loyal at the right price."

Kenzie pursed her lips. "Forty one?"

"You'd better believe it. And that's matured. Not necessarily mature."

He grinned through gap-teeth. Kenzie picked up his file from those gathered on her lap. Pearce had worked in many hot zones, from Grenada and Afghanistan to Syria and Israel. Undercover ops included Russia and China. But then so had so many others. Kenzie was looking for something different for her new crew, something stand-out.

"I'll be in touch. Next!"

She guessed auditioning a bunch of mercs in a relic smuggler's warehouse wasn't conventional, but it *was* Kenzie's bright idea, and a practice she quite liked the sound of. Since quitting SPEAR, and Torsten Dahl, she'd been moping around a hotel room, trying to decide what to do next.

For Kenzie, there was no other life.

She found herself settling back into old ways in less than a week. Calling old contacts. Hearing about new items coming to the market. The thrill returned, fusing her mind with fresh ideas. Maybe she could make a real business of this. Stop messing around with small scores and low payoffs, and start investing bigger.

That's why she needed a new—superior—crew.

The artifacts boxed and scattered around were inferior products. Objects taken by chance in the hope they might prove valuable. Many items ended up this way. Kenzie had borrowed the warehouse from an old friend for a few days and put the word out through every relic hunter and smuggler she knew. Every purchaser. Every evaluator.

She expected a few bad pennies, but what she seemed to have gotten was the entire arcade.

Reece, Jobson and then Trisk passed her by. Kenzie dismissed them, showing them the buffet table to her left as she judged the next. Only six remained. She started to think she might have to come up with a contingency plan.

"Dallas," the next said.

Kenzie looked up. He was dark-skinned with wiry muscles and a broad frame. His eyes studied her with intelligence. He didn't start to speak, but let her find his file. What she read was promising.

"You fought in Syria?" she asked, surprised. "With SPEAR?"

"Yeah, a lot of soldiers joined that battle."

"I won't pretend to remember you."

"Nor I you." The small grin was more than a little sarcastic.

Now Kenzie smiled. "And I see you spent time with Luther?"

"Again, true, although our units were eventually split."

Kenzie drifted away for a moment. Talk of Team SPEAR brought back a few nostalgic memories. Some of the best times of her life had been spent fighting alongside Dahl or Drake or Mai, even friggin' Alicia. She thought of them all with fondness.

"You okay?" Dallas asked.

"I never realized I was nostalgic until now."

"I'm kinda the same. Love me a good look through an old set of photos."

Kenzie nodded. Her early childhood had been the same. "I can barely remember those days."

Dallas shrugged. "Then your dad got it wrong. At home I have photo albums, CDs and flash drives full of memories. When I feel low, I take it back to the old days when my dad was young and wanted to make memories. From Disneyland to Death Valley. From Vegas to Waimea Canyon."

Kenzie held the man's eyes. "You're supposed to be regaling me with tales of your mercenary triumphs, not tricking me with reminiscences."

"No trick," Dallas said. "Just the truth. I wear it on the sleeve, girl. Better get used to it." He gave her a huge grin.

"Call me girl again, I dare you."

Dallas's grin faltered. "Ah, sorry. Got carried away. I guess at heart, I'm still a boy."

Kenzie let it slide. She wanted to hear more from this man. His confidence and his sincerity were intriguing. "One mission," she said. "Go."

"All right. One time my bud and I were cut off from the unit. We guessed there were at least fifty Taliban in the hills."

"Your bud," Kenzie interrupted. "Where is he now?"

"Ah, well . . . he's at home. Caught a frag grenade in the right leg. He'll never walk unassisted again."

Dallas bowed his head. Kenzie flicked a glance at the rest of the waiting mercs and saw only two with compassion in their eyes. For some reason, that bothered her. Before Dahl, it wouldn't have. She'd wouldn't have cared either way.

Before Dahl. Now there was a new memory benchmark.

And now there was *After Dahl.* What came next?

She waved Dallas forward and indicated the other two promising mercs. "Do you know either of those two guys?"

"Nope, sorry."

"Well, we have to—"

Two enormously loud explosions shook the warehouse. Kenzie gaped to see the front and right-side walls buckling. Steel plates warped as blocks and mortar crumbled. Sections collapsed and daylight streamed in. Dust clouds mushroomed through the interior, sweeping past Kenzie and the mercs.

"If one of you assholes brought your personal shit here, I will kill you myself!" she cried out as she moved.

The mercenaries were in uproar. The more capable ones dashed away from the explosions, looking for cover. Kenzie was already sheltered behind a large crate, watching the destroyed front and right side, trying to see what was coming.

"Any ideas?"

She was surprised to see Dallas crouched next to her. "About what? Lunch?"

"Oh, funny. No, I meant about who the fuck is attacking."

"No. But I guess we're getting close to finding out."

Two more explosions shook the massive warehouse. More sections of the walls buckled. Fire licked along the sheet metal up to the roof. Some of the crates were in flames, a sight that made Kenzie wince. "I'm gonna be in so much trouble for this."

"Can't see that it's your fault."

"Vitesse won't see it that way."

"Vitesse?"

"The guy that owns this place."

"Yeah, you're right. Let's get the hell outta here."

Before them, the warehouse's façade collapsed. The right wall distorted and then shook and crumbled. The remaining windows exploded. Kenzie winced to see the roof collapse too; metal struts, timbers and tiles crashing to the floor in a great mass of debris.

"Any weapons in these crates?" Dallas asked.

"Nothing that you would like," Kenzie snapped back.

They backed away from the sturdy crate they'd been crouched behind. Before them the ceiling stopped collapsing about a quarter of the way along the warehouse. As the din subsided, Kenzie heard a new ominous sound.

Helicopters.

She saw them now, through gaps and rough holes in the damaged right wall. Two midnight-black choppers hovered six feet above ground, allowing men to rappel down. She glimpsed flak jackets, guns and helmets. As they landed they ran toward the warehouse.

Turning to the mercs she shouted, "Enemy to the east."

Most of them took cover or broke boxes apart, looking for weapons. Some ran. Three even ran the wrong way, straight toward the enemy.

Kenzie and Dallas continued to back away. They were now three quarters down the length of the warehouse, moving from crate to crate.

Kenzie checked behind. "It's looking clear back there. If we—"

The main force surged into the warehouse, firing indiscriminately with their automatic weapons. The gunfire was loud and didn't let up for half a minute. Kenzie saw the mercenaries she'd been interviewing torn apart, falling to the ground. Eight men died. Others fell away, wounded.

Dallas turned a worried gaze on her. "They're killing everyone."

"I'm counting nine attackers."

"Roger that."

"We move, we're toast."

"Yup."

The gunmen advanced, unchallenged, running as a group and covering each other. Kenzie thought they moved well, but not flawlessly. She saw their mistakes, their weak links. "If I had a gun," she said to herself. "I could take half of them right now."

"Me too."

She turned an eye on Dallas. "Why are you still here?"

"What? I thought we were partners."

"Did I say you could work for me?"

"You were about to."

Kenzie took a deep breath and turned away. In a stroke of luck, two or three mercs had uncovered a box of old handguns inside a crate and were using them to keep the attackers at bay. The choppers had landed outside. Kenzie could see both pilots waiting, keeping in touch through their comms.

"We escape," she said. "Whilst these idiots keep each other busy."

Without waiting for a reply, she moved. Then the most bizarre thing happened. As she rose, one of the attackers noticed her and gesticulated. Kenzie heard his excited shouts:

"She's there! Right there! Go, go!"

Kenzie faltered a little. "Shit."

"They're here for you," Dallas said.

"Still wanna stay with me? If you slip between those two crates they won't notice you."

Dallas nodded. "Thanks."

Kenzie turned away from the American. Again, she was being pursued and didn't know why. Maybe these people hadn't gotten the memo that had pardoned her. Maybe they were old enemies. Or maybe they just didn't care.

She ran, expecting a bullet in the spine at any second. A crate loomed to the right. She veered her run behind it, using it for cover. Bullets slammed into the wood milliseconds later, shattering some of the timbers. A mountain of crates stood up ahead, lining the back of the warehouse and standing to the left of the rear exit. There was only one door and they would be ready for her to try it.

Instead, she veered again, racing across their line of fire and jumping among the mound of crates. More gunfire resounded around the warehouse. With a quick glance she saw some of the mercs shooting at the attackers. Two were down, which left seven. The rest of the mercs she'd interviewed were heading for a side door, leaving her to her fate.

No surprise.

Bullets peppered the crates to her left and right. Kenzie dove among them, spun and looked to see how much time she had. Another shock reverberated through her body.

Was that Dallas? *Shit, you mad bastard.*

The nostalgia-loving merc had hidden himself until the attackers bounded past and was now *chasing* them. They didn't know it, but he was right behind the last man. A bullet made Kenzie duck to safety and desperately try to see between badly stacked crates.

Dallas leapt and kicked the last man in the spine, sending him sprawling across the floor on his face. He stopped, whirled and scooped up the man's weapon, hefting it and pulling the trigger before anyone could react.

Five of the runners hadn't noticed.

Dallas shot the fallen man and then one more before he was targeted. He barely made it to cover, diving headfirst the last few feet. Kenzie stifled a loud cheer.

Five left.

What do they want from me?

They came fast. Knowing she stood no chance, she waited. Whoever planned this was good—they'd possessed knowledge only she had. Which meant they'd been watching her since she left SPEAR.

And she hadn't noticed.

The first man came around her crate. She grabbed his gun arm and twisted. He was a fighter, and ready for it, moving with the rotation and unbalancing her with a shoulder barge. She caught the blow on her face, blood drawn by the edge of his flak jacket. She kicked out the back of his legs, and held on to his gun as he stumbled. She managed to turn the barrel just as the second attacker appeared.

She shot him point blank in the face.

He flew back, gaining her precious seconds. The first attacker had hit the floor and was already rising, a hand hanging on to the gun. She saw the shadows of her attackers coming around the crates, pausing. She heard more gunfire.

Dallas.

A shadow fell. Another whirled away and engaged the American. Kenzie was left with the man on the floor and one coming around the crate. She felt the gun wrenched from her grip. She leapt clear, hitting the new attacker as he appeared, pushing him back and wrestling for his gun.

He shrugged her away. She flew across the floor, smashing into a crate with an impact that jarred her spine.

The man glared at her and brought his gun around. He couldn't attack because that would mean coming out into the open, and Dallas was still alive. But he could quite easily shoot her.

Kenzie saw her death before it happened. There was nothing she could do. Lying on her back, facing a bullet.

If only I'd stayed with SPEAR—

With Dahl.

Fleetingly, she wished for Dallas's sense of nostalgia right about then. What would her last thought have been?

The man in black opened fire.

CHAPTER EIGHTEEN

Crates shook and swayed. Columns tumbled. The entire array of heavy wooden boxes collapsed as Dallas threw his body at them. More importantly, two crashed down on the man targeting Kenzie as he fired.

A bullet rushed past her head, striking metal at her back. The man folded, losing his weapon. He wasn't done, though, just bloodied. Without taking a breath, he crawled from under the crate and reached for his gun. The second man—the one she'd fought first—was back on his knees after being struck over the head by another wooden container. Kenzie saw a brief ten seconds of breathing space.

It was enough.

The earlier metallic clang at her back had sounded familiar. She rose and turned at the same time. Swords gleamed at her feet. She knew these weapons.

Kenzie scooped up the best and ran back to the gunmen, reaching him as he lifted his gun. The black barrel swiveled toward her; the man rose to one knee. She saw no other option, and brought the sword blade down and through the man's wrist. The gun fell with the hand, leaving the man staring in horror at a bleeding stump.

Not for long. Kenzie brought the sword back on its return swing, slashing his throat. Without pause, she stalked past the dying body and used an upward swing to slice the face of her final opponent. He screamed, gun falling to the floor. Blood flooded his eyes and he saw no more as Kenzie dealt a last blow.

She heard movement and looked up.

Dallas was watching from atop one of the fallen crates.

"Damn, girl," he said. "I didn't see that one coming. That's some nasty shit."

Kenzie flicked the sword, shedding blood from the blade.

THE BLOOD KING LEGACY

"Girl?" she growled. "You're calling me that, right now?"

Dallas slid to the ground. "Sorry, it's just me. I'm not being condescending. Quickly—those guys in the choppers are gonna realize all their buds are dead. C'mon."

Together, they checked the warehouse, saw the coast was clear, and then cautiously exited via the rear door. The whirl of rotor blades continued to slam at the evening air. Kenzie ran to the right side of the building and peered around the corner.

"Just the pilots," she confirmed. "What time is it?"

"Seven-fifteen," Dallas said.

"Which makes it six-fifteen in the UK. I have to call Dahl."

"Who?"

"A guy from the SPEAR team. This has to be connected to them."

"Why?"

"Because nobody knew my plans. I've been alone, spoken to no one. That means I was followed, tracked every hour since I left them. Which brings it back to SPEAR."

"Got it."

"Good. Now, let's get rid of those fucking pilots."

CHAPTER NINETEEN

When they started seeing *Café* signs up ahead, Drake slowed. A café would offer a nice open space after the constricting corridors, a chance to engage the enemy. It would also afford their enemy the same opportunity.

He was thinking about Secret Service agents and choke points when there was movement ahead. It was one of the rear-guard agents, unable to stay still as the pain from a bullet wound wracked his body. By the time Drake reached him the man was dead, his blood pooling on the floor.

"Shit."

Another came limping back from the direction of the café. "I tried to stop them," he said. "These guys just swept us aside. Well trained, well-armed, impossible to divert from their purpose."

"Did you see Coburn?" Hayden asked.

"Yes, he's fine."

"Where they headed?" Alicia asked.

"Straight through the café," the man told them. "All of them."

Which told Drake there would be no traps, no snipers in waiting. But he couldn't rely on that. If this was a new Blood King—a pretender or a copycat—then they should be prepared for anything.

"Numbers?" Dahl asked.

"Twelve," came the firm reply. "None wounded."

"Call it in," Hayden told him; to the others she said, "Let's move out."

Drake approached the café entrance carefully, slowing where the corridor widened just before it. Half a dozen windows looked in, through which he saw the standard array of tables and chairs, a long worktop and a condiment station. It had been closed down as a precaution when the President's men commandeered the wing.

"There's an exit on the other side," he reported through the comms. "Moving."

"At your back." Dahl touched him on the shoulder. The two men ran low to the ground, opened the café door and slipped inside. Alicia and Hayden covered them through the windows. Drake raised his gun.

The café was only a hundred feet wide but there were several places an attacker might hide. Drake's senses were highly attuned. He saw movement—a bulk of blackness rising to the left, coming up from behind the counter, the gun out in front, the helmeted head exposed first.

With barely any readjustment he swiveled, took aim and fired. The bullet smashed through the helmet a millisecond later, sending the shooter staggering back into a wall and shooting into the air. Bullets ripped through the ceiling.

"One down," Drake said.

It slowed their progress, which was probably their enemy's intention. They checked for more enemies or explosive devices but found nothing. Dahl took a call.

"Kenzie?" he whispered with relief. "Are you okay?"

Drake let Molokai and Kinimaka pass him to take point as he listened to Dahl's conversation.

"You too?" Dahl closed his eyes. "Look, I'm sorry, but it's worse at this end." He told her about their casualties and then waited for her to recover.

"More corridors ahead," Kinimaka reported. "We're moving."

"Go."

Hayden and Alicia went next.

"We don't know," Dahl said into the cell phone. "Something out of Russia apparently. A new Blood King maybe."

Drake let Dahl go in front of him and covered the rear.

"Yeah, Kenzie, I know and I'm sorry. I'm not sure I agree with the idea of auditioning mercenaries but, hey, I guess that's you."

Alicia glanced back. "Interesting. Tell her I can think of more than one way to audition a merc."

Dahl gave her a stony glare. This wasn't the time, but Alicia, like Kenzie, couldn't help herself. It was their way of coping and it kept them sharp, on the edge.

To Kenzie he said, "Call me when you're close," and ended the call. "She's coming to London."

Kinimaka was making good time ahead. They couldn't see their quarry, but occasionally heard them. An errant shout, a smashed door.

After ten minutes, Molokai took point, easing the stress for Kinimaka. The leader had to check for trip wires, snipers and a thousand other potential traps. Molokai continued ahead for another fifteen minutes before straightening and holding up a fist.

"End of the line," he said.

Drake squinted into the low light. "Where'd they go?"

"Down."

CHAPTER TWENTY

Down and down, the stairs twisted. Dim wall lights were the only illumination, placed over twenty feet apart. The stairwell changed the whole dynamic of the chase. They could see and hear their enemy, but vice versa. Both groups were exposed.

But the SPEAR team couldn't risk firing a single shot in case they hit the President.

Drake checked the time: 6.20 p.m. Barely thirty minutes since they found the First Lady. What else was happening in London tonight? Had the President's kidnappers arranged anything else? Diversions, perhaps? The further he descended, the more detached he felt from the real world.

Three switchbacks and then three more. Drake guessed they had dropped three levels already so were approaching ground level. Was this their plan? To hit the streets of London running, having caused utter chaos?

In truth, he doubted it. Heading outside now would leave them exposed and their plan dependent upon pure chance. Molokai slowed to look over the handrail.

"Still going," he said. "They're in the sub levels now."

Drake raced past him, dropping two risers at a time. His weapon had four bullets remaining, but that didn't slow him down. His life revolved around keeping good people safe. Rarely had he or the other members of his team been targeted since they joined SPEAR. It usually only came as a consequence of the operation. But this . . . this was one more night of pure hell. Drake valued and trusted his team more than anything in the world; they were his family, his life.

The roster of murdered friends kept growing.

Drake shoved it to the side as he almost missed a step. Alicia was just behind. "You doing okay?"

"I'll be better when we retrieve Coburn and our hands on this latest killer."

"Won't be long," Alicia said.

"And find Karin," he added. "I wonder how Mai and Luther are doing?" There were so many friends in peril.

Molokai, keeping up his surveillance below, shouted, "Subbasement car park. They're heading into it."

Drake poured on the speed. This was it. If Coburn's kidnappers were trying to drive him out of here, they were going to get a nasty surprise. "Hurry," he said. "When we reach the car park, fan out, move forward. This is their first mistake. Let's punish them for it."

The last three flights took just a few seconds. The door banged below as the last of their enemy barged through. Drake eased up much as he dared, conscious of traps, but encountered nothing.

He halted at the door. "Ready?"

"Go." Dahl was at his back.

Together, they pushed through. Ahead, a dingy parking area opened out to both sides. Gray columns delineated parking spaces and marched in several rows to a far door about one hundred meters distant. An exit ramp stood to the left. Drake assessed the situation.

"It's good," Dahl said. "The ramp is the only way out and we're closer to it."

That's not right, Drake thought. *Their plan has been solid so far.*

In front, including the President, he counted twelve individuals on the run. He saw at least one woman running at the head of the pack and a man dressed differently to the others; a tall, lithe-looking man with cropped black hair.

Was this their leader? The so-called new Blood King?

It seemed unlikely. Drake switched his attention to Coburn. The President was being ushered along by two large men, both with a tight arm-lock on the head of state. Coburn looked to be struggling, but Drake saw a slump to his shoulders that made him think the man had been painfully persuaded to cooperate.

Several times.

Weapons bristled among the mass of men. Drake saw HKs, M60s and many others. He saw handguns and knives; grenades. The only person among them that was lightly armed was the tall man up front.

The SPEAR team advanced at pace, spreading out. When they were ready, Drake shouted, "Stop right there, wankers. First one to turn around gets a free third eye."

Whether they understood or not didn't matter at that point. Seven figures whirled, guns spraying lead across the entire parking area. Drake hit the floor. Bullets spewed. Several cars were hit, some of them bouncing with the force of the volley. Windows smashed. Tires blew. The team scattered, none of them daring to risk a shot.

"Wait," Dahl said. "We still have the advantage."

But Drake saw otherwise. "They're heading for that far door," he said. "Where does it go?"

Blank looks greeted the question. Karin would have known, he knew. Lauren would have known. Again, he fought off the sense of dreadful loss. They rose and crept forward as men surrounded the President and forced him through the far door. Weapons were aimed at the SPEAR team. Alicia rose to pick one of them off, but a well-aimed bullet smashed into the wall below her chin, sending her reeling backwards.

And then they were on their own.

As one they raced for the far door, noting it bore no sign, no exit sticker; only a handwritten sign that read: *Private*.

Halfway across the parking area, Drake's phone rang. "Yes?"

"Drake? It's Mai."

"Thank God. Where are you? We're on the bastards—"

"Just wait. There's more. Much more. Something big is about to happen."

"Something *big*?" Drake couldn't help it as his voice climbed several octaves. *"We're chasing the President's kidnappers through a basement car park with all gun's blazing. What the fuck?"*

"Calm down, soldier boy. We're close to you, but there's a strong, credible threat about an attack on London's CCTV headquarters. It's intense as hell out here."

"What?"

"It's not really a stroll through Disney Springs down here either," Alicia shouted back.

"Could be a bogus threat," Dahl said, "to divert attention."

"Nobody thinks so," Mai said. "This thing is big."

"Balls," Drake said, still running. "It has to be connected to the President and the First Lady. Surely it's a diversion."

They reached the far door. Molokai cracked it open and gave a signal. "Clear."

"We'll let you know. We're headed there now."

Drake closed his eyes for one brief second as he ended the call. What next? He didn't think he could take any more surprises tonight.

"A flight of stairs leads down to some subbasement level," Molokai said. "Moving."

It was narrow enough to prevent them descending in anything but single file. The steps were made of concrete, concave where their feet landed, and dusty. A few snack wrappers and pieces of shrinkwrap lay here and there. As they approached the bottom they saw another door—this one made of metal.

Service Area, a sign read.

On the other side was a wide, high tunnel, filled with machinery. Generators to help run the hospital. Air conditioning units. Boilers. A dozen other drab, gray humming hunks that whirred and buzzed with electricity.

Drake followed Dahl through the narrow path between them, listening for sounds of the enemy but hearing nothing above the din of the machinery.

At the far end another set of doors faced them. Once, they had been sealed with chains and padlocks, but those bonds had been cut. Dahl took a quick glance beyond then returned to confirm the suspicion that had begun to grow in Drake's mind.

"They're in the tunnels," he said. "The underground tunnels that dissect London."

"We lose them down there, we've lost them for good," Hayden said. "We have to hurry."

"And pray all is well up on the streets." Drake alluded to Mai's recent news. "Because, down there, we won't be able to contact anyone."

He turned to the door. Darkness beckoned.

CHAPTER TWENTY ONE

At the bottom of the stairs, they found a different type of passage. This one was unfinished. Roughly hewn, arched at the top, it resembled a London Underground tunnel without the train tracks.

Lamps attached to the wall above head height showed the way through. Drake wasn't sure if their attackers had fitted them or if they were permanent, possibly to help a maintenance crew. These tunnels led across the whole of London.

They crept along a curving passage. Arched alcoves lay to both sides, all of which had to be investigated. As Drake approached the third he saw movement.

"Don't—"

A head emerged from the darkness, followed by an arm holding a gun. Drake was quick to fire. Nevertheless, the attacker managed to shoot, the bullet whizzing between Dahl and Alicia. Drake fired three times before the man slumped dead to the ground.

"They're leaving gunmen behind to slow us up and thin us out," Hayden said. "Stay sharp, people."

"Sacrificing their own men," Molokai pointed out.

It struck a nerve with Drake. He walked another few minutes, checked another alcove and then stopped. "What the hell are we doing here?"

Hayden shook her head. "What do you mean?"

"I mean why are we here, now, when we should be up there? They killed Yorgi. Lauren. Smyth. Our great friends. And we're . . ."

He couldn't go on as a sense of overwhelming loss struck like a hammer. Yesterday, their friends had been happy, full of life and dreams. No doubt Lauren and Smyth, and probably Yorgi too, had been thinking about a future. A better future. Because of their loyalty, their friendship and their sacrifices, they had become a major part of Drake's life.

Of the whole SPEAR team's life.

He put his thoughts into words. "Our place is up there. With them. Looking after them, even in death. Let someone else lead this chase."

Hayden stared at him, mixed emotions flashing in her eyes. He knew what she wanted to say. She wanted to remind him that this was the President they were trying to save. Of what had happened to the First Lady, her agents, and the horrors her children had been subjected to. She wanted to emphasize the dreadful repercussions that would occur if any terrorist organization acquired him. But this was Drake. She knew how he thought.

"I agree," she said. "But what do we do?"

Drake gritted his teeth. She was appealing to his conscience. If they abandoned the chase now, if they capitulated to someone else, could they face the aftermath? Good or bad?

"I will clear out the next alcove," Molokai grunted and moved on. The newcomer knew he wasn't a part of this struggle.

"I know we should continue. Morally, it's right," Drake said. "But after all that we have done, don't you think we've earned the right to choose our friends first?"

Hayden spread her hands. "Yes," she said. "Yes, we have."

It wasn't any kind of base emotion that distressed him. Not fear or hatred. He hadn't lost his nerve. It was a mix of love, intense loss, regret and the thought of having to face a future without three of the best people in his life. The whereabouts of Karin was also unknown. Drake might be a soldier, a fighter, but at his core he loved and cared more for friends that had become family. He was finding it hard to let go of the grief, even for a minute.

"I feel it too," Dahl said. "I hate the thought of them lying out there. Alone. With no one beside them. I feel we shouldn't be ignoring their deaths."

"We're not ignoring their deaths," Hayden said.

"I know," Dahl went on. "And that's the point I want to make."

"Don't give me any shit about how they would want us to finish this," Drake said.

"I won't, but they would. And everything we feel for them, everything we want to say, it will be just as heartfelt tomorrow."

Drake closed his eyes, fighting the sorrow and the guilt. Ahead, Molokai was passing his third alcove, having cleaned vermin out of just one so far.

"Coburn has a family too," Alicia said. "Children."

Drake looked at her. He didn't expect indifference, but he had expected a toned-down witticism, a good point coated in Alicia's branded form of humor. Yes, she had changed over the last year. Yes, she had come to terms with her non-stop race for the next horizon, and she was working hard on that. But this—for Alicia—was deep.

"We can't let them down?" Drake felt her words cutting clean through his irresolute heart.

"We can't let them down," Alicia said.

"C'mon," he said. "Dahl's right. How we mourn is up to us. We can love them just as well tomorrow as we could today."

Molokai was far ahead, a bulky figure in the distance. Twice now, they'd heard gunshots and saw lifeless bodies as they sprinted past. It didn't take long to catch up.

"We good?" he asked.

"Yeah, I'll take point." Kinimaka went past.

"I heard noises just now. Figure we're a few minutes behind."

Kinimaka approached another alcove. Movement stopped him, but Hayden came around and fired four rapid shots. A body fell; a gun clattered to the floor. They moved on. The passage bent to the right. Rats scuttled at their side for a few seconds, making Alicia cringe. To her credit, she didn't say a word or turn her gun on them.

Progress.

Alcove after alcove passed by as they fast-walked the underground tunnel. Every lurker they killed gave them an extra weapon. Extra ammo. Ahead, a dark figure moved, stepping out far too early from his small niche. Drake saw and lined him up. Before he could fire they learned why he'd given himself away.

In the dim light, they saw a grenade being hurled at them.

Not for a second did they back down. Dahl set off like a sprinter, straight at their enemy and the tumbling bomb. With a deft hand he caught the grenade and flung it straight back before dropping to the floor.

"Cover!"

The explosion hit seconds later. Drake felt the pressure wave and ignored the percussive sound. A moment later they were up again, heading further into danger, testing the unknown.

Somewhere ahead, President Coburn fought for his life.

They couldn't let him fight alone.

CHAPTER TWENTY TWO

Mai shared a look with Luther as they approached the three-story, nondescript office building that was central command for London's extensive CCTV network.

"I hope they welcome us with open arms,"

"Oh yeah, they're gonna love it when two special ops soldiers walk in there and offer to help them do their jobs."

Mai passed through a revolving door and entered an airy lobby. The inside was cool and hushed. Three security guards sat at a desk in front of her, with several more positioned about the room. Mai saw they were all armed.

"Hello." She held out her SPEAR identification. "We've been sent to help."

Her words were designed to test the water. The comeback was as expected.

"I'm not sure what this is." A middle-aged man with sideburns glanced at her ID. "But I don't recognize it."

"Then run it through your system," Luther grumbled. "Stop being a prick."

The man blinked, either at the blunt reprisal or at Luther's mass, emphasized by the white shirt he wore that was clearly a size too small. When he stepped forward, the guard looked right and left for help.

"Umm. Give me a minute."

"You've heard about the threats." Mai didn't phrase it as a question. "The President. We're working with the Secret Service. Some of our guys are trying to catch Coburn's kidnappers even now. We need to know what you know."

"SPEAR," the man said. "I never heard of you." But he did pass the card through a scanner.

"Well?" Luther growled.

"It's coming back with high-priority clearance, but that's *American*. I'll have to run it up the chain."

Mai clenched her fists, frustrated. *"You don't have time."*

"Miss, I—"

"Don't 'Miss' me. I'm Mai Kitano. The threat is real and, if the President's kidnapping is anything to go by, it's gonna happen any minute. You need us up there."

"Why would the kidnapping be connected to the Hub?" One of the other guards came over, raising his eyes to signify upstairs.

Mai didn't want to drag this out. She took out her phone and called Cambridge. His answer was firm and immediate.

"Put me on with them."

She handed Sideburns the phone. A moment later he hung up and called one more person. When he'd finished he pointed to the left.

"Elevators are over there."

Mai dashed away, followed by Luther. They waited ten seconds and jumped inside. A short while later, the doors opened onto something else entirely.

She saw a large circular room. TV screens ran in an endless row above head height all the way around. There was a mish-mash of cubicles in the middle. Each cubicle contained somebody watching several TV screens, themselves split into smaller segments. The windows were blacked out. Mai noticed offices to the far side.

"C'mon,"

"Helluva first date, eh?"

Mai thought of those that had died. "Yes," she said.

"Ah, sorry, I didn't mean—"

"I know. It's okay. Let's concentrate on what's happening here."

Mai walked ahead. She knew Luther was only trying to keep up the pace, the rapport and the connection between them—knew he was trying to keep her focused. But she couldn't hide how she felt. The losses so far were life-changing for the survivors.

A broad-shouldered individual wearing a gray suit came

out of one of the offices to greet them. "Julian Reynolds," he said. "How can I help?"

"How far down do your eyes reach?" Mai asked.

Reynolds knew what she meant. "Not to subbasement level," he said. "And not to the tunnels. We do have eyes on every outlet though; the ones we know about and many *they* simply *can't*. We will see them the moment they emerge."

"What do you mean—there are cameras they *can't* know about?"

"There are many secret cameras in this city, Miss."

"And what of the new intel regarding an attack?" Luther asked.

"It's from a good source, via MI6. There's so much happening around London tonight . . ." He shook his head. "Maybe it's more misdirection."

"Where did the information originate?" Mai asked.

"Came from a guy called Wu," Reynolds told them. "A US deserter. Said he was working undercover for this Blood King character. A man called Luka, apparently. This Wu was attached to someone called Karin Blake, also a US deserter, and with ties to your team, I believe."

"Where is Wu now?" Mai asked, thinking of Karin.

"I'm sorry, he's dead. Found at a country lord's estate along with the lord and several staff. There were no signs of Karin Blake, or her partner, Dino. Now, I've helped you. How can you help me?"

Mai opened her mouth to explain, but a loud concussive blast almost knocked her off her feet. Luther saved Reynolds from falling. All three looked to their right.

"That's how," Luther growled.

Men and women were rising all around the room. Mai saw hundreds of scared faces. Guards were rushing to the windows.

"What the hell was that?" Reynolds asked.

"The beginning," Mai said.

Another blast shook the building. Mai saw a trail of fire

through the darkened glass. "Rockets," she said. "They're firing RPGs at the walls."

"But how did they *get them?*" Reynolds asked, perhaps straying from the point. "This is London."

"Influence. Money. Power. Threat," Luther said. "Incredible threat, with all the reach of a mid-size nation. It's never how many small or large grenades an enemy has smuggled into your country, it's whether they can find someone cunning enough to fine-tune the operation."

"That wasn't in the briefing." Reynolds backed away toward the center of the room.

"No," Luther said. "It never is."

A third and fourth blast hit in quick succession. Mai saw two trails of fire, both grenades falling short of the windows and striking the walls. She imagined the streets outside— enemies positioned in alleyways with rocket launchers over their shoulders, helpers loading the grenades. One man used earpieces to guide them as he watched from an elevated, secure location. Two more explosions rocked them, these far lower, the impact lessened.

"They just took out the entrance," Luther said. "Get away from the windows!" he shouted. "And get the fuck down."

Everyone whirled and ran. Mai rolled over two pairs of legs as another rocket hit just above the row of windows. It shattered glass nonetheless, sending mortar and whole bricks plummeting to the ground. Mai heard sirens. She was sure that this time the appearance of the police would help.

But they couldn't help right now. A rocket found its target, smashing into the frame that surrounded the windows and exploding.

A gout of flame surged inside. Deadly fragments sprayed the room. Partitions were shredded and collapsing. Fire consumed several TV screens, melting the plastic bodies and shattering the glass. Those screens above the windows sagged and then fell, breaking into pieces.

In the aftermath of the blast, people looked up.

"No!" Mai cried out. "Stay down."

Her warning saved lives as more devastating blasts struck the HQ. Mai felt the floor shake, saw the walls shuddering. She saw one rocket streak right inside and impact with the ceiling. Enormous bursts of orange flame and gusts of lethal debris detonated from the impact area. The ceiling buckled. Metal and timber crashed down onto those lying below. The screaming intensified.

Mai felt a steel sheet slam down onto her back, one of the metal panels that formed the false ceiling. Her shoulder blades took the force of it, bruised and bleeding, but she shrugged it off and sat up. The chance of another incoming missile was high, but she couldn't just lie there and take it. Luther was rolling to her side, putting out a fire in his shirt and checking his arm at the same time.

"Took a hit," he gasped. "But as I always say, 'if it's still attached, don't whine about it.'"

Mai pushed a thick length of timber off a woman's back and put out a small fire in an electrical circuit that was spreading between damaged cubicles. She rolled two women under a desk and forced a hysterical man back to the floor.

Luther concentrated on the other side of the central area. He crawled between remaining partitions, trying to calm the employees.

None of them were watching the CCTV screens.

And even if they were, Mai saw only about fifteen or twenty still functioning. She sought Reynolds in the rubble, grabbed his arm and held his eye. "Is there a backup? Do you have a backup station?"

"Yes, yes, there are numerous redundancies." He coughed, his mouth bloodied. "But none of them are this well manned. They're satellite stations."

Mai guessed it was time to call Drake. If the Blood King escaped those tunnels, nobody would see where he went.

The attackers in the streets below didn't care about anything but causing mayhem, taking the screens out and the backup down. They were hit again and again, yet there was no physical assault.

Mai and Luther rode it out, helping those that couldn't help themselves.

CHAPTER TWENTY THREE

Drake slowed.

They had reached the end of the long underground passage. It broadened ahead, becoming a wide chamber with a low ceiling. The lighting in the area was dim.

"Is that a—" Alicia began.

"Yeah," Kinimaka answered. "There's an old tube train ahead. Shit. The tracks must start right there."

"I really hope it doesn't work," Drake said.

Dahl moved faster. "Why else would they come here?"

Sensing this strategic and brilliant end to the kidnappers' plan, the team came together. As they approached the point where the tunnel widened, Drake saw movement ahead. The tube train was two carriages long. Near the front, he saw eight mercenaries carrying rifles and dressed similarly, a man and a woman wearing casual clothes with flak jackets strapped over their chests, and one more man—the guy he'd thought might be in charge. Beside him stood President Coburn, both hands tied behind his back.

"Best chance yet," Drake said. "Make it count."

They raced for the rear of the train. A shout went up ahead. All eight mercenaries spun and fired. Drake dived to the left, narrowly avoiding falling into the train-track pit. Kinimaka did fall in and let out a large bellow.

Dahl tapped the Yorkshireman's ankles. "Behind you."

Drake rolled out and fired back. His bullets strafed the walls, forcing their eight attackers to take cover behind the front of the train. The President was dragged inside by the unknown woman and man.

The tall leader stared back at him. "Matt Drake," he said and spat. "You will soon find the death that you deserve."

Drake answered with a bullet. The leader twisted away, jumping aboard the train. His lackeys popped up once more,

THE BLOOD KING LEGACY

aiming in Drake's direction. Bullets shattered the rear panel of the train, taking apart windows and metal, and bouncing off the iron wheels in a noisy hail of ricochets.

"Bet you wish you'd kept that grenade now," Alicia whispered to Dahl.

"I'm not sure even I could have found a pin to stick in it that fast."

"Really? But you could have used your—"

"We have to keep this cautious," Hayden interrupted. "Remember, any crossfire hits the President and we've lost."

Drake sighted under the train but couldn't see far enough to the front.

When Molokai leaned out to take a shot, a bullet whizzed past his head. "Stalemate. We're going nowhere."

"I'll forgive you for saying that," Dahl said. "Since you don't know me that well."

Within seconds he was climbing up the back window of the train, using its frame and some of the ragged edges to boost himself up. When he'd gained the roof, Dahl crouched low and looked down.

"Gun."

Drake handed him the most accurate weapon they had, with extra bullets. Dahl fell onto his stomach and crawled forward.

Molokai raised an eyebrow. "I'm guessing he does that a lot?"

"Yeah, he's nothing if he isn't a mad bastard," Drake replied.

They waited. Alicia half-climbed the back of the train to check his progress. Before he was halfway along they felt a shudder pass through the train.

"No," Hayden said. "Oh shit, it's about to—"

Drake held her back. "It's on Dahl now," he said. "He'll make it."

He held his breath. Molokai drew the kidnappers' attention with the occasional shot. Drake noticed the cobweb of scaly bumps and lesions that covered part of his face ran around the back of his shoulder and down to some point on his back. He looked away.

The train juddered as gunfire exploded from the front. Drake looked out to see Dahl leaning over the right side, loosing shots among the eight mercs. Two went down, unmoving, whilst two more twisted away, bleeding. Several weapons hit the floor. Drake picked off one of the wounded men that strayed too far from the train.

Dahl ducked to safety as return shots were fired.

Drake ran along the side of the train, closing the gap. Already, it was moving. Very slowly. Trying to pick up speed. He was faster.

Dahl rolled back into sight and fired another volley. One more merc collapsed. Drake saw four remaining and stopped to take aim. To his right, Molokai, Alicia and Hayden fanned out into the line of fire, their weapons ready.

From behind came the clatter of footsteps.

Drake almost whirled, finger pressing on the trigger, but Kinimaka's loud cry stopped him.

"No! It's Secret Service and British Police."

Good. They can help stop this friggin' train.

But the momentum was building. On top, Dahl was borne along, passing the mercenaries, heading for the tunnel ahead. If he didn't jump he would be crushed.

"Now!" Drake cried.

Secret Service and cops joined him as he, Alicia and Molokai ran forward, their weapons trained on the mercenaries.

"Don't move, don't move!" Hayden shouted at them.

Dahl jumped and hit the platform, landing on two feet and then rolling. He came up behind the mercs with his weapon held steady.

Drake approached. Out of the four enemies, two glared with incredible hatred. He wasn't surprised when one squeezed his gun's trigger. Four bullets struck him as he fired, sending the shot upward at the ceiling.

"We have three surviving mercs," Drake heard one of the Secret Service agents say into his comms system. "What do you want us to do with them?"

"Whatever you have to," came the quick, curt reply.

Drake watched the rear of the train disappear into the tunnel. It held only four people—the President, the orchestrator of all this chaos, another man and one woman.

"Where's it headed?" one of the cops asked. Drake recognized his SCO19 insignia. SCO19 were the British version of SWAT.

"Trafalgar Square," another answered as he consulted a map. "It's a very old service line to Trafalgar Square."

"And what does Trafalgar Square have?" Drake asked. "More tributaries than almost anywhere else in London," he added in answer. "More escape routes."

"We need eyes," the SCO19 cop said. "We need CCTV."

"Our team's working on that," Hayden said. "Maybe you guys can work on these men?"

The Secret Service agents were already pulling the three surviving mercs to the side. "Information," one said. "That's all we want, boys. Information on where they're going. How many? Who they are? Who coordinated all this? Everything."

"You think we should follow?" Alicia asked, staring down the tunnel with distaste. "We don't know what's down there."

"All the way to Trafalgar Square," Hayden said. "It's just a few miles."

"We can't quit now," Dahl said. "Follow me."

Together, they chased the darkness that chased the train.

CHAPTER TWENTY FOUR

Hayden struggled to detach from and sort through a minefield of mixed emotions. Of late, her feelings for Mano had been overwhelming. Their relaxing stay in London had only made them flourish, giving her a new purpose in life, offering up a different kind of future. They could be happy, she knew.

They could be happy forever.

It took some give and take, some sacrifice, some agreeing to disagree. It took commitment, respect, trust and belief. It took everything you had—but gave so much more back.

More interestingly, this cementing of their relationship had come as their team's future turned ambiguous. The President still wanted them. Secretary of Defense Crowe would move heaven and earth for them.

But they had been disavowed by the US Government. Hunted. On a kill list. They had no home—no headquarters. The promise of the secret HQ appeared to be without substance. Trust was in short supply. Add to this the team's various personal issues, Dahl's family problem, Kenzie's departure, and the deaths of their friends.

Where did that leave them?

Could they live apart, with their lovers, friends and families, and still come together as a team when the world needed them?

It was an interesting concept. Hayden knew it needed work. But she couldn't see a way for SPEAR to continue to exist as it did now. Their circumstances had changed. It was the end of a great era. Whatever came next had to be different, fresh, innovative.

Hayden was determined to make it happen. She saw a future for Drake and Alicia together, taking long weeks and months to relax, learning to live with each other. She saw

Dahl returning to the family life, making up with his wife, and treating his daughters to good family living and perhaps the occasional trip to Disneyworld. She also saw Dahl combatting his feelings for Kenzie, but that was a whole different story.

She saw Mai and Luther perhaps giving it a go. Maybe in America. Probably over in Japan, near Tokyo where Mai could spend time with Grace and her sister. Already, Hayden thought Luther would go with her. She saw Molokai being invited around their various houses, a traveling uncle or half-brother, which made her smile.

And that left Kinimaka and her. *What do I see?*

A chance for bliss. Peace. Togetherness. Accentuated by the non-stop, action-packed, incredibly dangerous life that they loved. Accentuated *occasionally* by, rather than dominated by.

It's the way forward, she thought. *Remember this. Mark my words. It is the way forward.*

Darkness crowded them. The cops handed over half a dozen flashlights. Hayden trained one on the floor, careful to walk between the tracks. There was no litter, just rubble—small and large stones, gravel and mounds of dust. And there were rats—the sound of their high-pitched squeaks grating on everyone's nerves. The tracks were dull.

Molokai led the way, stating he was used to picking his way through darkness. Nobody questioned him.

It was a long time before they found the train again.

Hayden fell in as Drake and Dahl took point. She felt better now as wall lights illuminated the way ahead. Her fingers were wrapped around a Glock supplied by a Secret Service agent.

Kinimaka whispered in her ear, "I got your back."

Drake and Dahl took a few seconds to declare the train empty. There were no clear footprints in the dust that covered the platform. Alicia was already focused on the exit.

She checked for traps, finding none. In front, the Englishwoman looked happy at taking her turn. Hayden came second. Yet another dark passage led to a set of stairs.

"We're going up," Alicia said.

Kinimaka was able to get a cell phone signal as they rose. "We're close to Trafalgar Square," he said, squinting at his GPS. "Probably coming up in one of the surrounding buildings."

They emerged into a subbasement, which widened just a few hundred feet in all directions and led to more stairs. Five minutes later, they arrived at a second subbasement.

With three exits.

"Shit." Alicia chose one at random and hit the stairs at a run. Soon, they emerged into a third basement, this one with four exits.

"They could be anywhere," Hayden said. "And have used any one of them."

"The police should be all over Trafalgar Square by now," Drake said.

"But were they fast enough?"

One more flight and they came up into a well-used basement which, judging by the scattered boxes and filing cabinets, belonged to an office block. They broke doors, set off alarms, and eventually reached a second-floor office with windows that stared out across the busy public square.

Standing beside each other, they looked down onto the architectural vista that was Trafalgar Square. Nelson's Column stood untouched among the bustle. Tourists walked, ambled and rushed from place to place, pausing to take photos and check out the black lions and fountains, with no clue that the best special ops team in the world was staring down at them.

A clutter of lights shone from every direction: traffic lights changing, shop lights glaring, flashing souvenir shops and car headlights, always on the move. People flowed across the road. Other monuments were lit in stark whites and emerald colors. Hayden saw hundreds of tourists sitting on the various steps.

An early rising moon illuminated the scene.

"Chaos," Kinimaka said.

"Yeah, it's not exactly Waikiki Beach," Alicia said.

"Oh, that can have its moments of madness, believe me."

"Not like this." Drake pressed a hand against the glass. "Down there is a madman, and he's got the President."

Police were everywhere, threading among the crowd, manning the crossings, even peering down from nearby buildings. Hayden saw them on the roofs, blocking intersections with their vehicles, talking to members of the crowd.

Drake's phone rang. Hayden watched him take the call. "Drake here," he said, switching to speakerphone.

"It's Mai." The Japanese woman sounded husky and reserved. "We've been hit. The CCTV headquarters I mean. It's bad. They pretty much took down the whole system."

"Are you okay?"

"Yeah, we're both fine apart from bruises. No casualties at all, which is a miracle. They hit the building with RPGs."

Hayden closed her eyes for a second, breathing deep. Were there no depths this new menace wouldn't sink to? She listened as Mai explained how everyone was pulling together to re-establish the feeds, but it was going to take some time.

"Meanwhile, the Blood King escaped the tunnels and used Trafalgar Square to cover his getaway," Drake said.

"We're calling him the Blood King now?" Mai asked.

"Whatever. It's easier than anything else. There is a bit of good news. We captured three of his mercs alive and the Secret Service is questioning them as we speak."

"Good. Shouldn't take long."

"So what's next?" Kinimaka pressed his forehead to the glass, staring at the multitudes below. They didn't have comms, so Hayden was forced to keep a sharp eye on the police. If they started moving fast, the chase would be back on.

"The feed might have caught them leaving the tunnels before it was destroyed," she told Mai. "Look out for that too."

"We're on it." The call ended.

Before Drake could replace his phone it rang again. Hayden watched as he frowned at the screen. "That's bizarre," he commented. "The incoming number begins +7. What the hell country is that?"

"Does it matter?" Dahl grumbled.

"Aye, it does, mate. I know every number, every call, that I get. At least, where it originates. This is . . ." he tailed off.

"Just answer the bloody thing," the Swede said.

Drake complied. Hayden watched his face. After a moment of listening he scratched his head. "Nothing," he said. "Just static."

"Probably a dodgy call center," Alicia said. "Just what we need now."

"At the end of it all we're just six people," Dahl muttered. "Well, five plus a Swedish superhero. If they don't spot him soon, we're done."

Hayden stared into the crowd as if her eyes had facial recognition installed. She knew the figures she was searching for. Their stances. Their clothes, although that information couldn't be relied upon. She knew Coburn. Were they still here?

In the silence, her mind revisited its earlier thoughts. Was SPEAR and its current method of working over? She saw different opportunities on the horizon. She moved closer to Kinimaka, brushing the big man's shoulder. He leaned in. It was so good to have even that sign of togetherness.

She didn't want to be alone anymore.

And neither, it seemed, did anyone else. It had been a long time since she thought of her father—JJ. The man had principals, integrity, and she'd tried living up to his deeds all her life. Now, she knew that, as a daughter, she didn't have to live up to anything. Through experience, Hayden had her own values, and needed to remain true to those. Everything else would follow.

"We should be out there," Dahl said.

"Normally, I'd agree," Alicia said. "But there's nothing we can do except wander around, hoping for a break. How often do you think that happens?"

"More than never."

Drake slammed the window in frustration. "We can't wait anymore," he said. "I'm calling the Secret Service. They've had enough time to break those mercs and we're dead up here."

Hayden agreed. "Do it."

His phone rang.

CHAPTER TWENTY FIVE

"We have information," the Secret Service agent said.

Drake tightened his grip on the phone. "We're listening."

"The person we're chasing is a man called Luka Kovalenko. He's the old Blood King's son. He blames both the United States and you guys for the death of his father. And I mean, to the point of fanaticism. He wants revenge. When Dmitry, his father, was killed, this Luka guy vanished. He knew that hidden nests of underworld leaders would slither out of their lairs and take apart his father's empire and that he wasn't strong enough to stop them. Luka is clever, a thinker. He watched it happen, then spent two years claiming every little bit back, surrounding himself with the right kind of killers, and presumably planning this attack. Our informants tell us that the plan went into overdrive when Luka heard about the old American embassy closing down."

Drake felt a deep anger. "I've never heard of Luka."

"Few have. But I seem to remember everyone initially believed the first Blood King was a myth. Why would anyone assume he had a son?"

"We need more background on him," Dahl said. "That could be the way to figuring out his plans."

"Agreed. There is some more. He arrived in the UK about a month ago but has been smuggling and stockpiling arms for a year. He took over a reclusive lord's country estate, one of those obscure ones that nobody knows about. Our captives tell me a woman called Karin joined their crew a few weeks ago, and that Luka turned on her tonight. According to the mercs, Karin called friends for assistance. One, a guy called Wu, was killed. The other, Dino, was taken along with her."

Drake swallowed drily. "Taken?"

"My merc wasn't privy to the details. All he knows is

they're being taken to a place called Devil's Island. Apparently, it's mega-important to Luka's broad plan."

"Is that where he intends to take President Coburn?" Dahl asked.

The agent sighed. "No, unfortunately. That, at least, would give us some time. We've found out something far worse."

Hayden grimaced. "Tell us."

"Luka Kovalenko intends to auction off the President. Literally, on the Dark Web. He has an auction contest set up for tonight. The highest bidder wins."

Drake swore, aggravated and feeling thwarted. "The guy's eight steps ahead of us," he said. "Do you have any idea where he's going?"

"No. These mercenaries weren't privy to any destination."

"Did you check the estate?" Molokai asked. "Maybe some of the more important mercs were left back there?"

"Everyone we caught is singing the same song. To be honest, it feels a bit prearranged to me."

"He's messing with us," Drake said. "Even through the captives."

"Some are saying they were coerced," the agent said. "After they signed on, their families were threatened. Isn't that how Dmitry used to do it?"

"Yes," Hayden said. "And Dmitry used to have camps where he kept hostages, slaves and workers. Have you checked the estate grounds?"

"Nothing like that there."

"It all feels orchestrated," Drake went on. "You can guarantee something else is gonna happen. We need to find this wanker." Frustration twisted his face.

"Luka infiltrated, outsmarted and overcame crime bosses. Oligarchs. Long established gang leaders. Some of them still don't know who he is. I'd say we're dead in the water until he decides what we're doing next."

Drake thanked the agent and ended the call. This inaction

wasn't good for his heart. Thoughts of Yorgi, Lauren and Smyth were creeping back in, weighing heavy. It was in everything he saw, everything in front of him. Memories everywhere.

To distract himself, he turned back to the window.

"Now we wait," he said.

CHAPTER TWENTY SIX

Luka Kovalenko took a moment to review everything that had happened so far. From the wounding of the First Lady, her breakneck rush to casualty, the assault on her room, the trip underground, and the journey on the old train. Every few minutes he'd received updates on events transpiring in London. He'd been informed the moment his men disabled the CCTV building.

By then, Luka, Topaz, Andrei and President Coburn were exiting a row of executive offices and stepping out into a brisk, bright London evening. Luka was happy with their progress, but every step of this operation was risky, and this moment was no different.

"Say anything, Mr. President, and we kill you right here. Right now. I also promise that I will kill your family. I reached them once, I could do so again. It's your choice."

Coburn stayed quiet, which pleased Luka. He snipped the President's wrist ties, letting them fall to the floor. Topaz, his bodyguard and Andrei, his father's enforcer, pointed ahead.

"We go to the right of Nelson's Column, and toward Charing Cross underground," Andrei said. "To meet the car."

This was the riskiest part of the plan. They could never be sure of the exact time they would emerge from the underground tunnels. Thus, a car couldn't drive around and around, waiting to collect them. The roads around Charing Cross railway station were busy; enabling them to blend in. Luka counted the minutes since the CCTV building was hit.

"We have a four-minute window before they flood this place with cops," he said. "Maybe less."

They hurried, but not enough to stand out. The pedestrian lights that allowed them across the road and to the center of Trafalgar Square were good to them, going green as they approached. The square itself was crammed with strangers.

Luka took the President's arm and helped him through.

"Keep your face down," Topaz growled.

"Sorry, I thought that might look odd since we're in sightseeing central right here."

Luka forged ahead. Couples, families and groups of schoolchildren barred his way. All three kidnappers were wearing black jackets and baseball caps, carrying weapons and coiled for instant action. Soon, they climbed the steps that led to the National Gallery, then switched direction, heading for Duncannon Street. The car was on Adelaide, just a short walk away.

Luka felt the pressure easing off. "You see what we can do?" he hissed into Coburn's ear. "You think you are so great. So powerful. But you see what we can do when we have real motive? I was forged when you killed my father. You created me. I hope you like what you wrought."

"Your father was a lunatic," Coburn said. "And so are you."

Luka barely refrained from lashing out, so outraged was he that Coburn could make so little of his life, all that he had become. All his father had grown to be. But it was exactly what Coburn wanted.

To grab some attention.

Instead, Luka whispered, "The car is ahead. I will enjoy selling you to the highest bidder."

Coburn stared at the medium-sized vehicle that waited. "A police car? You're kidding me."

"How else could we move freely tonight? Now, get in. It's not real, but it's real enough for what I need."

They climbed into the back seat along with Andrei. Topaz jumped into the front. The driver, wearing a police uniform, waited for the nod and then drove away.

Luka replaced Coburn's wrist ties. "Oh, and I thought it best not to mention it until now." He leaned back against the window as the car started negotiating London's busy streets and gave Coburn a large grin.

"Your family," he said. "They're going to die with you."

Coburn struggled, his face turning white. "No, you have me. Why would you need more?"

"Maybe because I'm a lunatic, Mr. President. But really, it's vengeance. I will pay you back for killing my father. You will wish you'd never discovered the Blood King. My plan is foolproof, so just sit back and come to terms with your fate. It all ends tonight."

With that, Luka turned away from the President and directed a question at Andrei in the center of the back seat. "Are the containers prepared?"

"Yes, Luka, they are. The occupants are uncomfortable, as requested."

"Perfect. And Karin in particular? She played a great part in destroying my father's empire."

Andrei nodded.

"The ship is ready to sail for Devil's Island?"

"It is. We're just waiting for the other two you requested."

"Don't worry, they will be along shortly." Luka laughed.

"You sound so pleased with yourself," Coburn said. "But you're causing mayhem, committing murder. Innocent people are being hurt."

"I am the Blood King," Luka said with disdain. "I do as I wish."

"And what is this island?"

"You're quizzing me for information? I assume you think you will survive then. I will tell you this, President Coburn. The island holds a great prize, a lethal secret, horrors that you can't imagine and a thousand deaths. Only the bravest survive there."

"You're talking about Vegas, surely?"

Luka watched as Andrei backhanded the man across the face. "I'm pleased that you remain spirited," he said. "I look forward to seeing that spirit crushed bit by bit, minute by minute. I look forward to your worst pain, Mr. President."

"Airport in ten minutes," the driver reported.

Luka sat back, satisfied. Nothing could stop them now.

CHAPTER TWENTY SEVEN

"It's nuts," Cambridge told them. "And bloody spooky too."

Drake could hardly believe his ears. "You're saying that every single captive started talking at exactly the same time?"

Cambridge appeared to suppress a shiver. "Yep. The ones down in the underground and the ones back at the lord's estate. All of them."

Drake shuddered. Cambridge had called and asked them to join him down on the street just five minutes ago. Now they were standing in an otherwise empty alley, huddled together, watching the world go past. The walls were so close on both sides, everyone was lounging against one.

"How long ago?"

"Minutes," Cambridge said. "I was already en route to Trafalgar Square."

"And what do they say?"

"That the President is aboard a flight to Paris."

Drake felt like pinching himself to see if he was dreaming. "A prearranged signal, I get that," he said. "The sudden talk gets the message across. But why tell us he's on a plane right now?"

"Well, it's not like we can shoot it down."

"The Blood King will not be vanishing into the shadows," Molokai said. "This night is not yet done."

"You think he has plans in Paris too?" Cambridge asked.

"It's a certainty," Dahl said.

"You got a plane we can borrow?" Alicia asked, raising an eyebrow.

"No plane," Cambridge answered. "But I do have helicopters. A whole fucking lot of them."

"The Blood King has a solid thirty minute lead on us," Hayden guessed. "That could put him close to being in the air. How far away are these helicopters?"

"Agent Jaye, they're right around the corner."

CHAPTER TWENTY EIGHT

The helicopters were in the air and thundering over London in less than fifteen minutes. Drake and the others got their first sight of the stricken CCTV building, marked by plumes of smoke that still streamed into the sky.

"We haven't heard anything from Luther," Molokai reminded everyone as they settled into their seats.

Drake called Mai and was informed the duo would be hot on their heels, chasing them across the skies to Paris.

"Perfect," Drake said. "We'll see you soon."

The helicopter swung through the night sky, buffeted by crosswinds, lit starkly by a shining, silver moon. They had been joined by a second chopper, this occupied by Cambridge and several SAS soldiers. A third was loading, being manned by a choice pick of the President's Secret Service staff.

"The French?" Drake had asked prior to boarding.

"Happy to help." Cambridge shrugged. "Considering the circumstances, they have no choice. They're ready for incoming, both in the air and on the ground."

"All we have to do is track the aircraft?" Hayden asked.

"Already done," Cambridge said and waved them off.

Now, Drake shrugged into Kevlar, arranged a Glock in his waistband and prepped a C8 carbine, the Secret Air Service's rifle of choice. Made in Canada, it replaced the esteemed M16 and is based on the ArmaLite Ar-15. Drake was used to it. Rails on the handguard allowed for extra lasers, grips and grenade launchers but Drake had access only to flashlights, one of which he slotted in right away. This was the bigger barreled gun, with a 15.7 inch barrel and a 30-round magazine. When he'd finished arranging everything to his satisfaction, he took a look around the cabin.

"Now we're ready for the bastard." Dahl grinned back at

him, holding up a C8 in each hand. An assortment of handguns and knives rested on his lap.

"Tooled up to the max and then some." Alicia hefted rifles and handguns, then threw grenades to everyone. "Get some."

Drake keyed his new comms system. "Cambridge? You read me?"

"Good to have you with us," Cambridge replied. "Some of the guys over here have heard of you."

"Oh, bollocks, send them my apologies."

"They've heard of Alicia too."

The blonde looked up. "Oh, shit, have I shagged any of them?"

"Why don't you tell me?"

"I dunno, it's a pretty big regiment."

Cambridge responded with a chuckle. "Nobody seems to remember it."

"Well, that's good. They'd remember. Believe me."

Drake broke it up. "You mentioned having a fix on Luka's plane? Where is it now?"

"Fifteen minutes ahead of you."

Hayden shook her head in surprise. "What? Why? What's the madman up to?"

"I wish I knew. All that's clear is he's not in a rush, they're flying safe and sound, and have made no demands. He knows he can't be shot down or interfered with, I guess, but that doesn't tell us what he has up his sleeve after landing."

"How far to Paris?"

"Forty minutes now."

"Then I guess it won't be long until we find out."

"One more thing has happened," Cambridge told them. "President Coburn has been allowed to speak to his generals, and only them. He's assured them that he's safe and will be released after they land. That's made it an even thornier problem for the US Government."

"Under duress," Drake said. "Has to be."

"I agree, but nothing's certain tonight."

Drake thanked Cambridge and made final preparations. The team were primed.

"One thing is certain," Hayden said. "We will save the President."

"And take the little bastard Blood King down," Dahl said. "That's certain too."

"For our friends," Alicia said.

"And everyone else he has hurt," Drake said. "Once we land in Paris, he isn't gonna know what hit him."

CHAPTER TWENTY NINE

Ahead, the pilots could see the Blood King's plane.

Drake moved over to the window and craned his neck. "I see lights," he said. "We're closing in."

"Only to where he wants us," Dahl said.

"Then the feeling's bloody mutual," Drake said. "I hope he wants us to see the whites of his eyes."

"Paris is on the horizon," the pilot said. "If something's going to happen it'll be soon."

With three British military helicopters in pursuit, hastily commandeered private jets fast catching up, and the French armed forces waiting to respond, Luka Kovalenko's plane came within sight of Paris. Drake could see the glittering sprawl down there, the golds and browns of houses and streets, the illuminated monuments and the dark snake of the Seine twisting its way through.

"How far's he gonna go?" Hayden wondered.

The answer came quickly. Drake watched as the plane veered to the right and started to descend.

Rapidly.

"It's going down," he said.

"What? It's crashing?" Alicia pulled him back and stuck her head in front of his.

Drake sighed.

The pilot came on again. "That's a fucking steep dive," he said. "I don't like the look of it."

Could Coburn have taken the plane Harrison Ford style? Drake shrugged the idea off. Although pleasant, he couldn't see it happening.

"He needs to pull up," the pilot said. "He really needs to pull the fuck up."

Drake saw it now. Kovalanko's jet was light, a six-seater. It looked like it was diving at the heart of Paris. Their own pilot followed as close as he could, but at a safer angle, cutting speed to keep the other jet in sight.

"No." Drake saw the Eiffel Tower ahead. "No, no."

Up here, he couldn't imagine the scene down there. But he did see a dozen choppers taking off. Fighter jets streaked through the skies. Tiny figures were running around below. The flashing lights of police cars swept the streets and buildings with multi-colored hues.

Every second, the scene grew clearer.

"A statement?" Dahl shook his head. "I don't believe it. The Blood King won't go out this way."

As if to prove his point, the plane leveled a little. It was still low, still badly angled, but its speed was lessening.

Drake stared, confused again. "What the hell is he doing?"

The plane turned hard in the sky, right wing lowering toward the ground as it dove in that direction. Drake saw the image of it outlined against the backdrop of the Eiffel Tower, a stunning and dreadful sight. It curved again, still descending, still dropping toward the busy streets of Paris. The skies bristled with choppers, from military to personal machines.

"He's at three hundred feet," the pilot reported. "Coming in hard."

Their helicopter descended rapidly, sending Drake's stomach into his mouth. They saw the underbelly of Kovalenko's plane, the angle leveling, the velocity reducing.

The pilot's next words were coated in disbelief and amazement, as if spoken against the man's will. "The mad bastard's going in for a landing."

A well-lit Parisian street grew large below. Drake didn't know which one but did spot that there were no parked cars. No shops. It was a private residential street in the heart of Paris.

"A mews?" Drake said, gripping the window frame to steady himself as winds buffeted the chopper.

"Plane is small," the pilot said. "If he's good he might

make the landing. No way will he stop in time though."

Drake's heart pounded for the President and the residents below. Their chopper hovered above, dropping steadily. The road was well lit, the surrounding streets thronged with tourists and famous hot-spots. He felt some relief that the madman Kovalenko hadn't decided to land among them.

As they watched, Kovalenko's plane crash landed into the Parisian street. It swooped at a low angle, cutting speed drastically before it hit. The front tire exploded. The plane wobbled, swerving one way and then the other. Smoke burst from the wheels as the rear tires hit tarmac. This impact steadied it and then the big jet engines kicked in, producing massive reverse thrust and severely slowing the plane.

It skidded forward at around fifty miles per hour, swaying and smoking. The right wing impacted with a streetlight, smashing it and bending the light. The collision sent the plane into a spin. Incredibly, Drake noticed, it helped slow it down too. The rear end brushed past a short row of residential windows, blowing them out, the heat melting part of their frames. The plane spun again, its pilot struggling to maintain some control. The far end of the street was coming up fast.

Drake watched. Their chopper hovered sideways and above the spectacle, ready to land as soon as it was safe. The plane's nose cone swiped another streetlight, bending significantly, but the plane had lost most of its momentum and was coming to a stop.

Wreckage littered the street in its wake. Small fires burned. House facades had been smashed or scratched. The plane itself was intact. It came to a hard, shuddering stop as its back end struck a wall.

"Down!" Hayden cried. "Hurry!"

They fell through the skies amid dozens of other choppers. Black ones, white ones, gray ones. They swooped toward the street, rotors thudding, on-board personnel grim and ready to act.

Drake thought he saw the other SAS chopper. A white streak blasted high overhead, the taillights of a French military jet fighter. Kovalenko's plane was immobile, its engines still blasting away. Drake could see right into the cockpit, but saw no movement.

Then the chopper's skids hit the ground. Doors were flung open. Alicia was first to land, boots striking terra firma, followed by Dahl. The Swede would be pissed at being second, Drake knew, and the thought gave him a brief warm feeling. He was out third, then Hayden and the others. Around them, more boots hit the deck.

"Steady," Hayden said through the comms. "There are an awful lot of variables here."

Kovalenko's plane shook. The door opened, and an inflatable escape chute was pushed out. Drake raised his gun, squinting along the sights. Everyone slowed and fanned out. It was one of the tensest moments of his life—dozens of armed men and women advancing on the Blood King's crashed airplane with the President aboard.

"Who the fuck's in charge out here?" Alicia whispered.

Dahl would have taken it, but Hayden spoke first. "Come out slowly," she yelled. "We need to see the President."

Still more choppers landed at their backs. The scene was loud and chaotic. But ahead, nothing moved.

Drake advanced one step at a time. To right and left, home-owners were staring out of their windows or twitching curtains aside. The soldiers waved at them to move back. Finally, there was activity ahead.

Behind the plane, at the end of the street, Drake remembered seeing an alley. Straining his ears, he heard the unmistakable shuffling sound of men running through it, toward the aircraft.

Good men? Or . . .

"No way," he whispered.

A gunshot rang out. It came from aboard the plane.

Hayden tensed. Drake felt his fingers clench around his

C8. A figure flew out of the open door of the plane, bouncing down the chute and landing at the bottom. For one long, horrifying moment the entire assemblage of soldiers held their breath.

Then Kovalenko leaned out of the open door. "Pilot," he moaned, grimacing in pain. "Fucker said he could land us safely anywhere on the planet. Fucker lied."

"Send out the President," Hayden shouted back. "Stand down, Kovalenko!"

"Ah, you know me now. That is good. I also know you. You are Jaye. The big one there is Kinimaka. And Drake, I spy a third walking corpse right there."

It was all Drake could do not to pull the trigger as images of Yorgi, Lauren and Smyth flashed before his eyes.

Kovalenko wiped blood from his face. "How about—you stand down. Otherwise, I will kill you all."

Drake wondered again if Kovalenko was running on a full set of cylinders. What the man proposed was impossible, and insane. But even he—standing with gun ready and fully focused—wasn't prepared for what happened next. Around the back of the plane, streaming along both sides came dozens of mercenaries.

Without hesitation, they opened fire.

Men screamed. Drake dived to the right, rolling fast. Behind, Kinimaka did the same, smashing into and destroying a big plant pot that one of the residents had left out in the street. A terrible firefight began.

French soldiers knelt and shot back. Hayden yelled for caution. Molokai scooted across the concrete to get a better angle on Kovalenko. Drake saw the Blood King disappear for a moment. He was replaced by the woman he'd seen earlier and another man, both gauging the escape chute with practiced eyes.

An endless volley of lead surrounded them. Drake picked off two mercenaries, but still they came running. French police and soldiers collapsed to all sides. An SAS man went down. Drake saw one the of Secret Service agents that had followed them here shot twice in the right shoulder as he attempted to run through hell to save his President. Behind him, Alicia caught a round in the vest and went down grunting.

Drake tried to pick more enemy figures off, keeping an eye on the plane.

"Don't worry," Alicia gasped. "I'm fine."

"Is there a problem?" he asked.

"Can't you hear me grunting?"

"Ah, I thought you'd seen David Boreanaz at one of the windows."

"What?" Alicia was suddenly animated, staring all around. "Where?"

"Get your head down." Molokai pressed her to the floor, still concentrating on the new attackers. "Are you mad?"

"I'm here aren't I?" Alicia fired shot after shot, trying to repel their closest adversaries.

"Speaking of mad," Dahl said. "I have an idea."

"Oh no," Drake groaned. "I hate it when you say that."

"Follow this," Dahl said.

Ahead, the chute bounced as two figures jumped out of the plane. Kovalenko appeared next and then another figure—a figure he held in place with a grip on the back of the neck.

And what looked like a gun nestled in his ribs.

President Coburn was hurled off the plane. The Blood King followed.

CHAPTER THIRTY

Dahl was up and running. He grabbed a wooden bench from a nearby garden, spun and hurled it high into the air, aiming for the mercs. They were bunched up, exchanging fire and losing men, the shock of their initial assault having passed. Some were falling back.

Drake saw why as Dahl's bench crashed down among them.

The President hit the bottom of the chute, and was grabbed by the woman and the other guy. Luka landed an instant later. The mercs were forming a half-circle around them, protecting them and, in the process, protecting themselves.

Return shots were aimed wide of Coburn. The Secret Service men were screaming for a ceasefire. Dahl's bench had knocked four men onto their backs and then the Swede was in their midst. He shoulder-barged one man high into the air, kicked another's knee out. He flung a third into the belly of the plane, displacing the metal. It was a valiant attack, but Luka and his followers were already onto the next step of their plan.

The Blood King ordered an assault. Drake counted twelve mercenaries break from the group and rush forward. Unable to use guns, the gathered French, Secret Service and SAS met them with knives and fists.

Drake rose to confront two men, Hayden and Kinimaka alongside. A knife flashed past his face. A gunshot came from one of the mercs, the bullet screaming past his ribs. He kneed the first in the sternum, then followed up with a right elbow to the jaw. Then he grabbed and flung the man into another shooter just as he fired again.

The bullet entered his colleague's body below the flak jacket, sending him flying to the floor. Drake grabbed his new opponent's gun arm as Kinimaka used a knife to finish him off. They let the body slump to the floor.

To their left was a crazy melee of bodies. Drake saw Secret Service agents trying to get around the crush. He glanced ahead.

He saw Dahl, Kovalenko and the President.

The Swede was being held back as Kovalenko signaled his remaining men to surround them. Drake was aware of the choppers hovering above, more soldiers climbing across the rooftops, and dozens pouring in from behind. A reverberant thunder of noise and commotion surrounded him. The screaming and shouting were non-stop.

"Do we have a point of contact?" he shouted.

Hayden shook her head. "Not on the French side, no."

"Do you see Cambridge?"

"We're fifty steps away from the President, Drake. We can't let him down."

We're doing everything we can. Under the circumstances, Drake thought they were doing well to hang onto the back of a plan years in the making. In any case, it was clear Kovalenko intended to use the alley as a getaway.

"Come on." He sighted on the mercs but then the President moved, and he lowered his gun. Dahl jumped in and out of sight, fighting two men. Alicia ran along a low wall to his right.

Kovalenko shouted, giving an order. Four men emerged from around the back of the plane where they had been waiting.

Drake saw what was about to happen. "Down," he cried. "Just get down."

Dahl flung himself sideways. Those men that heard Drake or saw the threat, dived and rolled, trying to protect their heads and bodies. Four RPGs were fired at once, rockets aimed at the surrounding house walls and into the battling soldiers. Two rockets impacted hard to left and right, striking brick. Two more smashed men out of the way before colliding with another building. The explosions were devastating. One of the facades crumbled. Flames erupted from the impact. Fire, bricks and deadly debris erupted from the walls. The attack felled almost everyone in the street.

Drake protected his head as wreckage rained down into the road. A bruising chunk of masonry bounced off his right hip. He saw an enormous, jagged chunk strike inches to the right of Molokai's skull. Shards from the impact rained over the man's head and shoulders.

Still prone, he looked ahead. Kovalenko and his comrades had disappeared around the back of the plane, probably running along the alley.

Drake rose, but this Blood King was proving to be every bit as crazy, as over-the-top and just as heartless as the old one. His grenade launchers had prepared a second attack.

Four more rockets flew, causing four more huge explosions. Choppers veered up and away in the skies above, almost caught in the blasts. Drake made the decision to stay exactly where he was. Now that the President was gone, he could focus on the four men holding him back.

He fired a shot as debris smashed down to his right. One man flew backward, dead, RPG tumbling away.

Alicia copied him, killing one more.

At the same time, bullets slammed into the other two, fired from the group of SAS soldiers and Secret Service agents.

The way forward was clear. Drake rose as fires burned around him, as masonry and glass shattered down into the street, as helicopters strained to fly over the nightmare scene. He saw his friends getting up too, heroes rising from the battlefield.

He tapped the comms, unable to shout. "Everyone okay?"

They sounded off one by one. They were ready.

Drake ran along the length of the plane. He passed the dying RPG shooters, and kicked a gun away from one of the men's questing fingers. They bypassed the chute that dropped down from the open plane door.

They saw the narrow, gloomy alley that led away. It was arched, built of brick, and empty.

Hayden hurried in first. Drake, the rest of the SPEAR team, the SAS and the President's Secret Service were next.

CHAPTER THIRTY ONE

If the Blood King planned on losing them in Paris's streets he'd miscalculated. Drake imagined the crash landing was where it all went wrong for Kovalenko and his goons—which was why he'd murdered the pilot—but even now, he appeared to have a backup plan.

They emerged onto the Boulevard de Clichy, in Paris's red-light district. It was a wide road, tree-lined in part. Lurid reds, yellows and blues shone from the façades of various buildings, illuminating the skies, the street and the passersby. Vehicles traveled both ways along the road. Drake ran out into the center, squinting ahead.

"Bollocks, I don't see them."

"To the left." Dahl indicated the sidewalk just past a sex shop sign. "Stop squinting, man, makes you look old."

"Well, sorry my eyes weren't immediately drawn to the big, red *Adult* sign."

"Sorry's not good enough," Alicia said, moving past. "You gotta work on that, Drakey."

"Please." He followed. "Please someone, stop her going inside."

"Oh, don't worry I won't," she said. "We'll visit afterwards."

Dahl and Molokai were ahead, hitting the sidewalk running. Hayden and Kinimaka followed, with Drake and Alicia bringing up the rear. Everyone kept their eyes peeled for surprises as well as firmly on the runners ahead. They knew how Kovalenko worked.

Coburn was being manhandled along the sidewalk, not far ahead now.

Molokai had stopped, lining the woman up in his sights. "Stop there!"

"Shoot to kill," Hayden said, through the comms. "No mercy."

The woman paused, whirled and threw a grenade their way. Parked cars provided adequate shelter as the bomb went off.

Drake peered back around a high wheel arch. A shop frontage had been destroyed, its windows shattered. Alarm bells wailed.

"What the hell is the protocol here?" he wondered aloud. "Much more of this and civilians are gonna get killed."

"The Secret Service will want Coburn at all costs," Hayden said. "The French? I don't know if there will be any protocol for this situation."

"And SPEAR?"

"As usual, we're here to protect and save civilians. But we want Coburn too."

Drake shook his head. "Thanks, love. That's clear as mud."

Figures were gathering behind them. Drake was sure Kovalenko would be able to see the force that was following him. Did he have anything else planned? Some last-ditch strategy? Of course, on the other hand—he'd wanted to be in Paris all along.

Up ahead, Drake saw a façade with shimmering white lettering and a golden windmill above. He recognized the place, and was shocked when Kovalenko and his entourage darted left, right through its front doors.

"Not good," Dahl said. "That is not good."

It gave the pursuers a chance to turn on the speed. Within a few minutes they reached the same doors, standing outside the world-renowned Moulin Rouge.

"Get on the phone," Drake said. "Clear this place—"

Bullets were fired from inside, slamming through the front doors. Glass shattered over him. An impact just below his chest forced the air out of him. He went down like a stone, gasping for breath. Around him, the others dived and rolled for cover.

Alicia grabbed his leg and pulled him clear. "Drake?"

"Yeah, yeah. I'm good." He could barely breathe.

"You're making weird gasping noises, Drakey. What's up? Did Dahl unbutton his pants again?"

Drake rolled clear. "Touché," he said. "Now help me the fuck up. I want to get in on this."

Secret Service agents, the French military and SAS soldiers were storming the front of the Moulin Rouge. The shooting had stopped. They leapt through broken window frames into the front lobby, Dahl and Molokai among them. They crunched through glass and dropped to one knee, guns ready. They fanned out across the inner space.

Drake saw a display of souvenir windmills, cakes and stacks of cocktail glasses standing to the right. Incredibly, the precarious stack of glasses was unscathed.

To the right, a line of pay booths stood empty. But Drake heard the sound of terrified breathing.

"Sound the evac," several men shouted at once, some in French. "Sound the alarm now!"

Heads bobbed up, staring like deer caught in the headlights, too terrified to do anything. A second later Kinimaka walked clumsily into the stack of glasses that had survived the barrage of bullets, sending every single one crashing to the ground.

"Crap."

The noise galvanized the tellers. One reached for the panic button. The others ran for the door.

Drake joined the main group as they crept further into the theater. Inside, it was a mix of deep, rich colors, illuminated by brass and steel lamps. The carpets were plush, the fittings expensive looking. Drake voiced his thoughts through the comms.

"I think Kovalenko's gonna get beyond the theater, then use firepower to empty it out, sending the patrons straight at us. That's his exit strategy."

"Agreed," Hayden said. "We have to move faster."

An explosion shook the building. The team raced forward.

A moment's silence followed before the screaming began. Doors were flung open; doors that led to the main theater.

Drake passed them at pace and saw a large, opulent main room, full of well-dressed, well-groomed men and women. Eyes were wide and staring. Some were running. Some were waiting. Still others appeared to be in shock.

"Keep going!" Dahl shouted from behind. Drake's chest was pounding where the bullet had hit, but he sucked it up and drove his body faster. There was no choice. They had to get past the theater exit or would lose the President in the rush.

Terrified patrons were already among them. Drake couldn't blame them. He sidestepped around two men and a woman. Ahead, a stream of people erupted from the final set of doors.

Drake was engulfed. He tried hard not to hurt anyone, not to trip anyone. He moved toward the far wall, pressing through the crowd.

"Try every door," Hayden growled.

Alicia cut left into the emptying theater. Molokai followed her. Drake broke free of the surge of people, stopping in an empty corridor that wound toward the theater's back end. Dahl was at his side.

"Hey," a female voice said. "What the fuck's going on, Torsten?"

Drake and Dahl whirled, dumbstruck as they came face to face with Kenzie and a black man. Drake saw the Swede's mouth fall open in shock.

"How . . . what . . . ?"

"Simple." Kenzie spoke fast and seriously. "I told you we would meet you in London. On the way we diverted to Paris after hearing the news. It's closer. Here we are."

Dahl nodded. "That's pretty simple. Who's the sidekick?"

"Ah, this is Dallas. He's just tagging along. I'm not even paying him."

"I didn't ask."

"Hey," Dallas butted in. "That's not what we—"

"Choose a door," Dahl said, indicating those ahead. "You got weapons?"

"Thought you'd never ask." She took his Glock. Drake offered one of his own to Dallas. As he passed he glanced into the theater.

"Can't wait to see Alicia's reaction when she sees you, Kenzie."

The Israeli grunted. "Any ideas where this Blood King asshole is?"

"Close by," Drake said. "And becoming more desperate by the second."

"How did he escape you guys in London?"

"The underground tunnels," Dahl said, walking on. "He had them prepped. Even had a train waiting."

Kenzie stopped. "Are you fucking stupid?"

Dahl turned to her. "Something on your mind?"

"I'd say. Here we are in one of the oldest sections of Paris, in a building from the late 1800s, standing in a city famous for its . . ." She paused.

Dahl closed his eyes. "Shit," he said. "We're so caught up in the chase we didn't stop to think. Of course, there'll be tunnels underneath here too."

Drake used the comms to spread the word. Hayden asked for help, hoping to find someone that might be acquainted with the theater or the tunnel system. Local cops would be their best chance.

"Quite a few of us here," someone answered her call, speaking in a thick French accent. "We're on your six."

Drake grinned as he waited. The Frenchman testing American slang out sounded somehow wrong. They waited just a minute.

Kenzie tapped Dahl on the arm. "How's the ball and chain?"

The Swede grimaced. "Nothing has changed in the short time since you left."

"Shame."

Around them, the Moulin Rouge shuddered.

CHAPTER THIRTY TWO

Alicia came sprinting out of the theater, bellowing at the top of her voice. "Run, run! Kovalenko planted people in the audience. They're strapped with explosives and dead-man's triggers. They were just fucking sat there like zombies, waiting for us."

Then she spied Kenzie. "*What the fuck?*"

Drake took a fast look behind her. Three men wearing heavy jackets, sweat running down their faces, and grasping what looked like a hand-grip were walking up the aisles. A fiery, smoking patch of ground near the stage showed where one man had already detonated.

Molokai filled his vision. "Can't fight them, can't shoot them," he said. "They're here for you, Drake. Us."

It was a terrible moment. Drake could have killed all three in as many seconds, but the theater would be destroyed; maybe the devastation would spread to other parts, killing innocent people or bringing the roof down onto soldier's heads. The SPEAR team headed backstage. Hayden and Kenzie were at the rear, with Dallas and Kinimaka close by.

Three suicide bombers emerged through the theater doors.

Drake ran behind Dahl and Molokai. They passed numerous closed doors, all bearing a star and a person's name. Gold leaf and red plush filled his vision ahead. A figure stepped out of a door, staring wildly. Dahl managed to propel him back inside and slam the door in his wake without slowing down.

"Is there an exit at the back?" Hayden spoke into the comms.

"Yes, past the dressing rooms and just after the props area. Look for a green exit sign to your right, at the side of a lighting tower."

"Okay. Our only chance is to get these crazies out into the open before we kill them. Clear the entire area out back."

"We're on it."

They hurdled props that had been left lying around, turned a corner, and hurried down another corridor. They gained a lead, as the bombers weren't running. Dahl and Molokai forged ahead. Hayden and Kenzie hung back a little to keep an eye on their pursuers.

Hayden called the Secret Service agents. "What do you have in the catacombs?"

"Lots of traps. Snipers. We're in the basement now. Kovalenko is somewhere ahead of us."

"We'll join you soon."

Drake came around the last corner to hear Dahl bellowing. Ahead was a wide space, littered with old props, piles of clothes, broken lighting racks and old chairs. To the right of a lighting tower he saw the glowing green exit sign.

Dahl was standing before it, hitting the push bar that opened the door. The whole frame wouldn't budge. It had been chained and wedged *from the outside.*

Dahl pushed with everything he had. Molokai took over but didn't do any better, and so did Kinimaka. Drake looked back as Hayden came into sight back up the long corridor.

"What's happening?" she asked over the comms.

"Door's locked," Alicia said. "It's a trap."

"Oh, God, they're only minutes behind." She jumped onto the communications system again, appealing for men outside to undo the rear door.

Drake took a breath and readied himself. If they were trapped in here, their best chance was to shoot the bombers as soon as they appeared. There was a last door at their end of the corridor, which he pointed out to the rear guard.

"Might as well jump inside," he said. "Should shield some of the blast."

"But you . . ." Hayden locked eyes with Drake, with Kinimaka.

They were too far away to join her.

"Don't worry about us. We'll be fine."

Her look showed she didn't believe him. Of course, she was right. He could hear the suicide bombers now, breathing harshly, gasping, their shuffling footsteps the nightmarish indicator of a slow-approaching, horrible death.

Hayden, Kenzie and Dallas slipped inside the last room.

Drake heard shouting. He whipped his head around to see Dahl's enormous frame and Molokai's huge bulk almost locked together. As one they ran, launching themselves at the exit door. The metal bulged outward, the frame shuddered. Both men fell to their knees, bloodied and bruised.

Still, the door rebuffed them. Drake felt helpless. There was no way out of this one. Alicia hefted her weapon, glared around as if she could force fate into showing her a second exit door, and then met Drake's eyes.

"Thoughts?" she asked.

Dahl and Molokai heaved themselves to their feet, cursing with pain. The exit door stood resolute before them.

"I definitely felt something give," Molokai grunted.

"I think that was my shoulder," Dahl said.

Drake turned his attention to Alicia, ready to speak his final thoughts. The shambling footsteps were almost upon them, the first of the suicide bombers approaching the end of the corridor.

"I know that I—" he began, but then a horrible shadow caught his eye.

The first of them came into sight, a sweating, hunched wreck. It was a woman with long black hair that hung in a limp, knotted bundle. Despite the large vest packed with dynamite across her chest, it was her eyes that Drake saw first.

Wide as saucers, white, terrified.

"Get this thing off me," she begged. "Please, I . . . I don't want this."

She was tugging at the vest as she walked. Drake rushed

at her and peered around her shoulder, back up the corridor. The other two had just come into sight, maybe a minute away. *Was there a chance?* He doubted it, the variables were complicated.

He pulled the woman out of sight of the corridor and asked Alicia to close her own hand around the woman's hand that held the dead man's trigger.

Alicia winced but complied, now as responsible for the bomb as the woman, as Drake. Dahl and Molokai watched with bated breath just a few steps away.

Alicia locked eyes with the woman, but shouted at them from the corner of her mouth. "What the fuck are you two doing? Stop hugging and find us a way out of here."

Drake studied the mechanism fastening the vest around the woman's waist. Four ratchet straps were positioned at her spine. There was no way she could escape it without help. He started unfastening the vest.

An almighty smash made his heart leap. Looking up, he saw Dahl and Molokai, again locked together, again charging the door like two battling rhinos. This time, the frame buckled, the door shifted. A gap to the outside became visible.

He made the fastest and most difficult decision he'd ever made. "Hayden!" he cried. "*Run, now!*"

Everything happened at once. Hayden and the others crashed out of the room as if they'd been listening with their ears at the door. Drake undid the last strap and ran to the edge of the corridor. Drake and Molokai gathered all their strength, ignored the pain, and attacked the exit door one final time.

Everything was riding on this final act.

Drake's faith was proven as they smashed into the door with their combined weight, tearing it off its hinges. They fell through, enlarging the gap. The frame collapsed, bits of the adjacent brick wall falling with it. Drake hefted the vest and threw it back up the corridor.

As one, they sprinted for the door. Hayden was already passing through, followed by Kinimaka and Dallas, then Kenzie and Alicia, who was dragging the woman by the arm, almost lifting her off her feet. Drake was last, but he heard the vest he'd thrown hit the floor. He knew when the approaching feet stopped.

"Now!"

Alicia threw the dead-man's trigger to the ground.

The blast was horrendous, a thing from nightmares. The saving grace was that the theater had long since been evacuated and almost every door was closed. The blast was contained inside the building, but a small portion of flame, an energy wave, and a rush of debris poured out into the night.

Drake was mid-leap when the energy wave hit. He felt it push at his haunches as if trying to give a helping hand. Nevertheless, it sent him awry, tumbling into the street and rolling against Dahl. He struck with a crunch and groaned. Before they could recover, flames rushed after them and licked up toward the skies, followed by debris. They were fortunate the building stopped most of the blast, because all three explosions were huge.

Drake pushed away from Dahl. The Swede nursed a dozen bruises.

"Next time you're trying to get away from an explosive," Drake said. "Put some bloody effort into it."

"Piss off, Drake."

He rose to his knees and took in the scene. Wreckage from the detonation littered the wide alley where they'd emerged. Some of it covered Kinimaka's legs and Hayden's arm, but both seemed okay. Alicia was sitting with her back to the far wall, staring up at the rear of the famous theater.

"Fuck," she said. "You guys just broke the Moulin Rouge."

As Drake turned, a portion of the roof collapsed, a wall sagged. Fighting their weariness and their aches, the team backed off down the alley, heading for the front. Behind them, part of the theater crashed down.

They paused at the top of the alley.

"What now?" Kenzie breathed.

"The Blood King is well ahead of us," Drake said. "But we still have the comms and contact with the men chasing him."

"Yeah," Dahl said, eyeing the broken roof and walls of the theater. "Back in."

Hayden nodded. "Back in."

As one, they rushed around to the front doors.

CHAPTER THIRTY THREE

Battling through dust, rubble and deadly hazards, they worked their way back to the staircase that led to the tunnels. Fortunately, it was closer to the front of the building and not subject to the damage that had been wrought at the rear.

Drake hammered down the steps.

Hayden shouted over the comms system, "Where are you now?"

"We've been heading in an easterly direction for about twenty minutes through twisting tunnels. The bastards are thinning us out. I've lost four men so far, all wounded, which is a blessing. We're forced to slow. We're not losing much ground, so they must be sticking together ahead."

It made sense, Drake knew. The Blood King had few allies now. Just the man and the woman. Was Luka worried or did he have more men waiting at the other end of the tunnels?

The whole team picked up speed as they reached a level surface. Their radio-guide had mentioned twisting tunnels but these snaked hard, switching back and around. Without a compass the team would never have known they were heading east.

But where to?

The journey passed in silence. The tunnels wound. Garbage lay strewn across the floors along with the occasional person. Drake saw needles and tiny plastic packets everywhere. He saw the remains of dens, rotted cardboard and long-forgotten belongings. He saw rats in the walls, chewing and creeping along. The stench down here was nauseating.

Minute by minute, they were closing in on their prey.

A little later, Hayden radioed again. "How we doing, guys?"

"Still here. The passages are rising now, though. We're headed back to street level."

Drake felt a surge of trepidation. The worst of it was knowing that this was part of the Blood King's convoluted plan. Perhaps a backup, or a Plan C, but even so . . . the man remained at least one step ahead.

As they ran, they prepped their weapons, rearranged their bulletproof vests, and tried to ease out their bruises.

Kenzie ran close to Dahl. "Good job with the door back there. Glad you were around."

"He's *lucky* he's still here," Drake said. "We only keep him around for the entertainment factor."

"Yeah," Alicia said. "And stay away from him, bitch. Stop trying to butter him up."

Kenzie looked confused, almost running into a sharply bending wall. "Butter him up? I am not into that at all."

"It's a bloody saying. Means to ingratiate yourself with someone. Rub them up the right way."

"Ah," Kenzie nodded. "Now, *that*, I don't mind."

Hayden was in front. Drake felt the passage rising beneath his feet. In another few minutes they would come up behind the assortment of French police and Secret Service agents that had been tracking the Blood King through the catacombs.

"Slow going," one of the agents reported. "We're guessing he's ten minutes ahead now."

Hayden nodded. "Anyone know how far below street level we are?"

"I've been trying to gauge that," a French accent answered her. "I figure they could be at the surface now."

"And do we know where?"

"Oh yes," the Secret Service agent answered. "We've radioed it in already. We're coming up under Gare du Nord."

Drake clenched his fists. "Shit, isn't that the busiest railway station in Europe?"

"Yep, which is why Kovalenko landed near the Moulin Rouge, emptied the whole place to cover his escape, and then used the tunnels *under* it to reach the station. This guy is as clever as he is ruthless."

Dahl swore.

"You have men in the station?" Kinimaka asked.

"I only just called it in," came the quiet answer. "But they won't just send men. They'll send everything."

"Good," Drake said. "Overwhelming force. Let's play this bell end at his own game."

The path rose, becoming steeper. The route continued to bend this way and that. There were no more traps, reinforcing the theory that the Blood King had exited the tunnels. Finally, they came to a high, wide, steel exit door.

One of the Secret Service agents stepped forward. The man was focused entirely on retrieving his boss. With a shove he forced the door open. Instantly, a vast hubbub assaulted their ears and, when they emerged, their eyes too. They were right outside Gare du Nord, opposite the peaked concrete façade. A white, illuminated clock face sat in the middle. Cars and buses passed by the front as civilians thronged the entrance, moving in and out at various speeds.

Drake stood for a moment in the night, taking it all in. The others surrounded him. In addition to the eight-strong SPEAR team, they were joined by three Secret Service agents and four French police. The route across the car park to the front doors was temporarily clear.

"No sign of help," Drake said.

"It won't be long," a cop answered.

"Let's go."

Hayden led the way, the agents and Kinimaka at her back. Drake and Alicia fanned out to the right; Dahl and Molokai to the left, covering the main group in case the Blood King had prepared any surprises.

As Drake ran, his cell rang. "Drake here."

"It's Mai. We just landed at Charles de Gaulle. Where are you?"

"Gare du Nord," Drake said. "Is Luther with you?"

"Yes, we're together."

Drake smiled into the darkness. This would be a great

advantage. "Get here as fast as you can," he said.

"Don't worry. They laid a helicopter on for us."

His smile turned into a grin. He pocketed the phone. "Help's on its way," he said.

They reached the front doors, unable to keep a low profile among the mass of civilians. Some looked alarmed. Some hurried away from the station. Others gazed in suspicion, and still more reached for cell phones. The French police urged them to safety.

Inside, Gare du Nord resembled most other train stations around the globe, but with a Parisian twist. Drake saw a vast vaulted ceiling, rows of lavishly lit shops to both sides, and a host of trains, tracks and platforms running down the center. A wide walkway stood before him. The place was awash with noise and movement.

"Pretty sure they'll be traveling together," Hayden said. "Look, the chances of us spotting them among this crowd are ludicrous. You have to close the station, stop every train."

"It's already happening."

Six trains sat idling at platforms. Passengers strolled or sprinted down the length of at least four, trying to make it in time or grab a better seat from those less able to run. Nowhere did he see the suspects he sought. To a man and woman, they swept the station with their gazes from an elevated position, but came up with nothing.

"We have people on the trains now," the French cop reported. "Choppers inbound. Along with the Army. They will not escape this."

"With all these people around," Hayden said. "You could have a bloodbath on your hands."

"We are moments away from the evacuation."

Drake stared, ready for anything; any unusual movements. The seconds ticked down, dripping with tension.

Anything could happen. From a sighting of the Blood King or the President, to a rush of mercenaries, to an influx of people with explosive vests.

And still, he was shocked at what came next.

CHAPTER THIRTY FOUR

An announcement proclaimed the evacuation of the station; then the sharp report of gunshots drowned it out.

Drake saw passengers falling off a train, the third from the left. *They aren't falling,* he amended. *They're being pushed.* Men and women went sprawling, landing on their heads, their chests, their backs and faces. First two, then four and six. Many more. Amid it all, Drake saw the woman and the man, Luka's lieutenants maybe, leaping down among them.

"Do we know who those two are?" he asked. It would help to know what they were up against.

"Yes, they were identified through facial rec. Both had a violent criminal life before they joined Luka. The woman is known as Topaz, a Russian assassin-come-bodyguard. The man is Andrei, an enforcer to the old Blood King. Luka must have recruited them both when his father died."

"Tough dudes then," Kinimaka said.

"As hard as they get."

"We'll come back to you on that." Dahl leapt onto the handrail and vaulted over, feet first, landing eight feet below onto the main walkway that ran the length of the platforms. Everyone followed. Both Topaz and Andrei were right ahead, and now Luka could be seen leaning out of the train, throwing a figure onto the platform.

That's Coburn!

As soon as he landed, the President rolled and tried to run. Drake could see his face, bloodied and determined. A gunshot was fired, the bullet glancing off the platform by his feet, but the President didn't bat an eye. He kept running. Hayden and the Secret Service agents were pelting toward him.

Behind the President, a woman screamed. A shot was

fired over his head. Cursing, he whirled, and saw the revolver pointed at a passenger's head.

"Get back here," Luka shouted. "Or her death is on you."

Coburn slowed. Drake was in the second pack of runners. Their pace didn't slacken as they raced down the long platform, trying to reach the President in time.

The Secret Service agents were already aiming, judging distances and chance and reason. It didn't help when hundreds of passengers jumped off the train and rushed straight at them.

"*Fuck!*" Hayden yelled, readjusting her sights through the bobbing crowd.

Luka grabbed the President and dragged him back. Topaz and Andrei sprinted toward the front of the train.

"What the hell are they doing?" Kenzie shouted.

Drake heard a squawk of noise coming from the cops' radios, announcing that the military had arrived. Choppers were in the air. More police and SWAT units were converging on the station.

"It's a shut down," he said. "Luka's going nowhere."

"Yeah?" Alicia shot back. "Well, maybe someone better tell *him* that."

As the running passenger horde started to thin, and those thrown from the stationary train got to their knees, Topaz and Andrei jumped back on the train. His friends shared the sudden confusion he felt, voicing questions, but he concentrated on Luka.

It was his best view of the new Blood King yet. This man looked younger, less heavy, and far fitter than Dmitry Kovalenko, but Drake could see the similarities. The genes appeared to have been passed on in every way possible. Luka wrenched at Coburn's arm, forcing the President at the open train door, just one compartment from the front.

A Secret Service agent fired. The bullet glanced off the side of the train. If they could stop Luka now, they could reclaim Coburn. It was a five-second window. Three more shots rang out, bypassing the President by inches.

The problem was, the agents were still wary of Luka's position in relation to Coburn.

One bullet smashed glass, the second struck so close to Luka's head that he ducked and cursed. The third flew in through the open door where he stood. A second later he wrenched Coburn through and slammed it shut.

Drake stared from that door to where Topaz and Andrei had climbed aboard, just a compartment ahead. For a second he couldn't figure out their intentions. He didn't believe the Blood King was going to surrender, nor that this would turn into a hostage situation. What else could there be?

The entire chasing pack slowed when the train rumbled forward.

"Bollocks," Drake shouted.

"There is still nowhere to go," the French cop shouted. "We have men outside, choppers in the air."

But nobody among the SPEAR team would risk losing the President now. Alicia jumped onto the slow-moving vehicle, grabbing a door handle. Kenzie clutched a window ledge and clung on. In a typical Dahl maneuver, the mad Swede leapt from a window ledge to the top of the train, scrambling over the edge.

"Does Dahl ever board a train normally?" Alicia yelled. "Or is it always through the roof?"

Drake grinned as he kept pace with the train. Hayden was at the head of the Secret Service agents, Kinimaka a step behind. They were passing the fourth car from the front of the train, but it was picking up momentum, approaching the end of the platform, about to leave the station.

They had just a few seconds to decide.

Hayden glanced back, seeing those hanging off the train. Drake grabbed a free space too. The ledges weren't wide, and they were risky, but he couldn't leave anything to chance. He had to stay with the President and the Blood King.

Molokai clambered up to Dahl, as did Kenzie a moment

later. Dallas stared at her and then shouted, "Fuck that. I don't climb moving vehicles."

"It'll come out of your pay," Kenzie called down.

"Whatever, I haven't seen a cent yet."

Drake tended to agree with the climbing maxim. Dahl was running up top, falling headlong but managing to grab the sides to hang on. The others were crawling or crab-walking in his wake. Dahl leapt across one small gap, gaining the second car from the front. The train jolted over a link in the track. Dahl fell again, slithering toward the edge.

"Gotcha!" Kenzie leapt and grabbed his arm. Molokai took hold of her legs and dragged them both back into the center of the roof.

"Move with caution, proceed with grace," the large, mysterious man told them. "Do what I do."

Dahl looked dubious, especially since the words were coming from Molokai, but proceeded ahead with a slight let up in pace. Drake saw the front of the train pass the platform's end.

Three Secret Service agents had made it to the front. They slammed their guns against the door Luka had dragged the President through, smashing the glass. One looped an arm through the gap, fumbling with the door. Another pointed his gun at the empty space, backing his colleague up. From within came a fleeting movement. A knife appeared in the first agent's arm, making him scream. His legs kicked but he managed to hold on. His colleague tried to sight Luka.

The agent hung on. A shot came from inside, the bullet striking the second agent in the chest. He fell back, hit in the vest but not injured.

Luka popped up and wrenched on the knife that still stuck out of the first agent's arm.

The man screamed and fell away, crumpling to the platform, narrowly missing being sucked into the gap between its edge and the train's wheels. The third agent, now desperate, lunged at the door.

Luka rose and fired point blank. Drake heard him scream: "Get the hell off my train!"

It pulled clear of the station. Hayden managed to scramble her way onto another ledge, hanging by the tips of four fingers. None of them would be able to hang on for long.

Outside the station, craziness awaited.

CHAPTER THIRTY FIVE

Choppers hung in the air, some sweeping toward the train, others tracking it. Armed men hung from the doors and the skids. The train picked up speed out of the station.

As one, the helicopters swooped to follow.

It became clear that Luka had at least one final trick up his sleeve. He'd positioned more men at Gare du Nord. Posing as passengers they had initially followed him on to the train. Drake spotted them as the train flowed faster and the choppers took flight in pursuit. He also saw the flashing lights of police vehicles tracking them through the closest Parisian streets, and soldiers waiting by high verges to both sides, perhaps positioned in case they could jump aboard a slow-moving train.

But this one was traveling at speed.

On the roof, Dahl and the others had been forced to lie down and crawl. They were over the first car, trying to reach the center where a hatch was situated.

Drake, still hanging to the outside, saw four windows break ahead, and four arms push out. He saw basic handguns and four new faces, peering up into the air and then back along the length of the train.

Shit, they're gonna pick us off.

Hayden clearly thought the same, using comms to alert one of the choppers. A crimson colored one swooped in, taking the gunmen's attention as it swung at the train. At the last minute it veered, opening up its side where police marksmen lay. Shots rang out. The Blood King's men leapt to cover, although the shots went purposely high.

Drake turned his attention to his own predicament. Using his revolver's handle, he slammed at the nearest window, causing a crack in the glass and then smashing it. Alicia shot hers to pieces. Hayden and Kinimaka did the same. The chopper continued racing alongside them as the police lined up better shots.

Dahl reached the roof hatch and gripped the edges with his fingers. His chest heaved with exertion. The slightest raising of his head sent gusts of wind slamming into his face. He felt a tap on his ankle. Kenzie was ready.

"I jump," he yelled back to her. "You lean down and shoot. Molokai can hold on to your legs. Go it?"

"Yeah, sounds great."

Dahl tightened his fingers around the hatch.

Drake heaved his body onto the window ledge, preparing to fall inside. He heard gunshots and froze, thinking they might be aimed his way, but soon realized they were being fired upwards. At Dahl.

Hayden saw it too and keyed the comms.

Dahl saw an exit hole appear a few inches to the right of his head. He hadn't even tried to pop the latch yet. Another came close to his right elbow. Kenzie pulled away as a third exploded right before her eyes. Dahl could barely move, couldn't escape fast enough to avoid the row of bullets. Already, it was nearing his body. He shuffled back only just in time to avoid a bullet to the chest, pure luck letting him twist the right way.

Lying on his back, he glanced down the train. Kenzie and Molokai were stuck in a similar predicament. It was only a matter of time before one of them caught a bullet. There was a deafening roar as a helicopter veered over to them and plunged downward. It fell hard, stopping mere feet above the train. Its skids were just out of reach. Dahl jumped, aware the wind would take him to the right, caught hold of a skid and held on. A bullet struck the underside of the chopper. Kenzie grabbed the rear of the same skid Dahl held, and Molokai grasped the one on the other side.

As soon as they were off the train, the chopper veered away.

Hanging on, Dahl keyed his comms. "Keep us here, guys. Keep us close by. I don't wanna lose touch with the train."

The chopper kept pace, about four cars from the front and ten feet to the right of the speeding train.

Drake couldn't help but fall inside the train, landing on his ass. There was no grace, just the need to get in. He landed hard and rolled. In the aisle, he could see down the center of the train, most of the way to the front. So far, they were clear, but it wouldn't take long for their enemies to realize they were inside.

Dahl clung to the skid before wrapping his legs around it and rolling himself over so that he sat on top. Clinging to a cross-strut, he got a clear view of the chase. The train sped through Paris, passing the Stade de France, briefly following the curve of the Seine to the left before swinging to the right. As the train shifted so did the helicopters above, swerving and swaying with the train, tracking it around every bend and over every bridge. To their right, police chase vehicles kept pace, speeding through the streets of Paris, their lurid lights reflecting off the dark hulls of the choppers.

Dahl saw a chance and directed the chopper back over the top of the train. He'd seen Drake and Alicia enter and assumed they'd captured their enemies' attention. The pilot did as he was asked, and hovered over the speeding carriage as it slammed at top speed through Paris. It was forced to rise as a bridge appeared, its skids scraping past the bridge's guardrail, its body passing smoothly between two upraised concrete stanchions. Dahl heard men crying out in shock but held on. He could see ahead.

"Now," he said.

And they were back on the top of the train, landing deftly and lying prone, stationed over the top of the hatch.

He keyed the comms. "We're ready up here."

High grass verges engulfed them from both sides. There was a low bridge ahead. The helicopter roared as it veered away. Dahl dropped prone to the roof of the train.

Drake blinked as full darkness seemed to rush up against the windows. They were approaching a tunnel.

This is it.

Time to attack.

CHAPTER THIRTY SIX

The train braked. It decelerated so suddenly and without any warning, that Drake and Alicia shot forward, falling to the floor and rolling into seat backs to left and right of the aisle. Drake held on to his gun. Alicia lost and reclaimed hers in seconds. Together they gripped anything that came to hand as the train driver applied full brakes. Wheels squealed, and shattered glass skidded forward.

Hayden, halfway through her window, fell inside and rolled forward, reaching for a stable surface to halt her tumble. Kinimaka was worse off, finding himself thrown from a window across a double seat and then into the footwell. Drake was happy to hear the Hawaiian cursing. It proved he was unharmed.

Dallas and one of the Secret Service agents were still hanging on outside. Drake tried in vain to crawl toward them, fearing for their safety. But somehow, they hung on.

Up top, Dahl fought the momentum, gripping the edges of the hatch. Kenzie had grabbed his ankles when the driver braked, and hung on, thankful the track was arrow-straight and that she wasn't being thrown to the side. Molokai managed to grip one edge of the train and her left ankle. His grip was like iron.

It felt as if entire minutes had passed, but they all knew it was mere seconds. Dahl saw choppers overshooting the bridge and trying to swing around as best they could. He even heard cars squealing to a stop on the adjacent roads.

The train stopped.

They were surrounded by high grass verges. Drake couldn't see a tunnel ahead, nor a bridge above, but had to assume they were there. To his count, Luka, Topaz and Andrei had been joined by four more gunmen in the forward carriage.

He saw the Secret Service agent and Dallas jump from the train, and glared at the window he'd smashed. "I just got through that bastard."

Kinimaka groaned ahead and rolled out into the aisle. "I feel your pain times a hundred, brah."

Hayden was at the Hawaiian's side. "You okay, Mano? You took a big fall."

"I will be after a week on the beach."

Drake was on his feet, Alicia too. With Hayden leading, they raced down the length of their carriage, entered the third in line and ran down that one too. As they reached the second, they slowed, but a new sound caught their attention.

Gunfire from outside.

Drake ran to the window. Hayden and Kinimaka went for the open door. On the badly lit, sloping grass banks outside, men fought and fired their weapons. Andrei was battling the Secret Service agent as Dallas took on one of the mercs. Floodlights streamed down from the choppers, lighting it all in stark silver, but they didn't stay still. They were in constant motion, casting shadows and throwing the whole scene first into light and then into shadow.

Drake saw Dahl leap from the top of the train, roll and come up running. It was a tough feat, since the ground sloped so sharply. Hayden and Kinimaka leapt out of the train. Drake ran to the door, a step behind Alicia. To the far left, Luka and the President stood halfway up the verge, Topaz before them.

At their backs was a low concrete bridge, covered in vegetation. It looked unused, just an undemolished throwback to a previous age. Still, underneath it was a black world of impenetrable shadow.

Molokai landed heavily to the right. Kenzie was climbing down, poised above Drake's head. The SPEAR team were assembled and ready to charge. Luka Kovalenko was all out of chances.

They attacked the Blood King. They couldn't fire for he

stood in front of the President, who had been tied hand and foot and thrown to the ground. The three mercenaries came at them from the right.

Alicia dropped to the ground, firing at the same time they did. Her bullet took one in the vest. Drake covered the ground faster, reaching the mercs and driving among them.

Kenzie was at his side.

She dove and rolled, then struck with her feet. A merc staggered backward too fast to keep his balance. She was on him before he could move. A swift punch to the throat made him buck and throw her off. Drake elbowed a man and ducked as a knife was thrust at him. Dahl was then at his side, taking hold of the guy and lifting him before depositing him onto his back. Drake spotted the remaining Secret Service agent go down under Andrei's vicious assault and diverted his attention that way.

The grass verge was a battleground as they sought to save and protect the President.

Choppers tried to land, thought better of it, and drifted away a few hundred feet to a flat area of land. Men and women jumped clear, racing toward the fight. Drake fought toe to toe with Andrei. The middle-aged enforcer was a tough prospect, used to battle and dealing out harsh punishment. Pain didn't affect him. Three heavy blows only made him wince. His return attack sent Drake staggering back several steps as he tried to cover up.

Luka stood, covered by Topaz, just to the right of the battle, the President tied and lying between them.

Drake had no time to wonder about such craziness, the impetuousness of it. Andrei battered him, forcing him back. To the right, Dahl had slipped and was falling back down the slope. Dallas was on his knees, trying to help Kenzie. The muddy grass incline wasn't helping their attack, as the mercs had the high ground. Alicia came up behind him, looking for a way to launch an attack. Drake slipped in mud, going down face first. Alicia took a blow to the face.

Across the other side of the tracks, those that had jumped out of the choppers were starting to climb over the high fence that guarded the railway tracks. As Drake spun he saw familiar faces and knew then that the tide was about to turn. His heart leapt.

All right!

Mai and Luther were here. They landed feet first, and ran down the far verge, across the tracks and up to join the battle. Mai was screaming as she hit Andrei, striking him about the face and skull, sending him reeling back. Body blows sent him to one knee. Drake spat mud and grass out of his mouth. He saw Luther smash full pelt into a merc, breaking bones, carrying him beyond Dahl and throwing him into another fence. The entire length of wood paneling juddered. The merc didn't get back up.

All the mercenaries were down. Mai was engaging every scrap of Andrei's attention. He was now fighting on his knees.

Drake looked to Luka.

It left just the Blood King and Topaz facing the SPEAR team and the newly arrived soldiers. For the first time today, Drake came within speaking distance of the young Kovalenko.

"Let the President go."

Luka watched Mai send Andrei sprawling, saw the Japanese woman render him unconscious. Then he turned to Drake. "It is not over yet. I have big plans for all of you."

Drake hesitated, aware of the Blood King's scheming so far. He worried that the train had been stopped on purpose.

"Give up now," he said. "And they might not send you to a black site for the rest of your life."

President Coburn was attempting to slither down the slope. Luka took a moment to haul him back up. "My life is just beginning," Kovalenko said. "And so is the worst part of yours. Topaz—give them a taste."

Without warning the scarred, almost-bald woman

exploded into action. She reached Drake first, but the Yorkshireman was ready for her. He blocked two blows, falling back. A third brought blood from his lower lip.

"Stand aside," a deep voice intoned. "We'll deal with her."

Luther and Molokai stepped up to the battle, engaging Topaz blow for blow, dealing out as good as they were given. The tall assassin was forced to up her game, putting everything into the fight.

Which left Drake and Hayden only ten feet from the Blood King.

"No more talking," Hayden said. "Get down on your knees, asshole."

There was movement in the shadows under the bridge. Four men appeared, melting out of the blackness, all dressed in gray suits. At the same time Luka unzipped his own jacket and took out a handgun.

"You think I stopped the train by accident? No, my disciples are waiting. Right here. Step forward, my disciples."

Drake stood rooted to the spot. The four men in gray suits were breathing easily, smiling. They approached the Blood King without hesitation. And, as they approached, they unbuttoned their jackets.

All four carried state-of-the-art automatic weapons.

They surrounded the Blood King and President Coburn, and took aim.

CHAPTER THIRTY SEVEN

The Blood King grinned at Drake.

"There are eight of you right here, not counting those playing with Topaz. And all from the great SPEAR team. Do you think you can take all four of these disciples before they fill your precious President full of American-made lead?"

Drake was coiled, ready to spring, only feet away from Kovalenko. The others were ranged to left and right. A quick glance showed that they were ready. The disciples watched through the sights of their barrels, aiming at Coburn. The President himself stared at the unfolding scene, which changed with every passing second: More men arrived, more choppers thundered, adding to the sound of sirens racing down a dirt track that probably led right to the abandoned bridge.

Drake checked on Luther and Molokai. The pair were struggling with Topaz, stronger but far slower, unable to contain her lightning attacks. Mai would have been a better opponent, but now she was right here alongside him, facing this new Blood King.

Kenzie was thinking along the same lines. She attacked Topaz just as the woman buried stiffened fingers into Luther's abdomen, making him fold. Kenzie looked odd, attacking without swords, but delivered two severe punches that made Topaz grimace. The Russian reeled away, snarling. Kenzie pressed her advantage but soon discovered she'd been led into a trap. As she pounced, Topaz darted to the side and spun with her right leg extended.

The force of the blow sent Kenzie sprawling, gasping, to the ground.

"What do you want, Kovalenko?" Hayden asked. "Is this your great plan?"

The Blood King gave her a rueful glare. "Whilst the plan is

foolproof, I had to rely on . . . certain individuals who did not measure up. But they are dead now. So . . . we go on. I'd love to chat longer, but I do believe that will come later."

Hayden readied her weapon. "Later?"

Alicia put it more succinctly. "How the fuck do you plan to escape, you fucking Russian fruitcake?"

"I will let your President go."

Drake felt a spark of hope but refused to let it overpower his focus. "Then do it," he said without emotion.

"Let me go," Luka said. "Right now, right here. And I will let the President live."

"Go where?" Kinimaka asked. "There's nowhere to hide."

But the Blood King was staring past them now. "Tell those men to stop moving right now."

The disciples heard the warning tone in his voice, and tightened their fingers on their triggers.

Hayden held up a hand. "Stop."

Drake turned to see a mixture of French soldiers and police approaching. "Lower your weapons," he said.

"Good," Kovalenko said. "I will tell you all something—this is not over."

"Let President Coburn walk free," Hayden said. "And then you go too. If that's what you want—I will honor it."

Drake swallowed. Hayden had made the only decision she could—but it was massively controversial. Kovalenko had killed people on English soil, on French soil, and even Russia wanted a piece of him.

A frozen moment in time stretched before them. To break it, Dahl leaned in the direction of the ongoing tussle with Topaz. "You want some help with her, boys?"

"No," Luther's voice was strained. "No, dude, we . . . got this."

"Why would you orchestrate all this and then let Coburn walk free?" Kinimaka asked the question that had been hovering around the forefront of Drake's mind.

"Because, at some point, I want him to die with his family."

The words were spoken without a flicker of emotion but hit the SPEAR team like shards of ice. This man, this underworld figure, was made of nothing but undiluted evil.

"I don't believe that will happen," Hayden said. "But hand him over now and walk away. If you can."

Drake was waiting for a request—maybe a fast car or a chopper. Kovalenko smiled. He took a moment to study the bridge at his back as if trying to penetrate the shadows underneath.

"I walk, you stay. My disciples will cover your President until I am clear."

In a twist of fate, Topaz managed to loop an arm around Luther's neck and throw him toward Kovalenko. One of the disciples diverted his attention from the President and trained his weapon on Luther. The big man froze just feet away from the unwavering barrel.

The Blood King also hesitated, a smile playing around his lips. "Well, that changes things slightly. I have a new deal. I give you Coburn if you let me walk away . . . and my man shoots this American pig."

Drake took a step forward. Topaz broke free of Molokai and leapt over to Kovalenko's side. She withdrew a Glock from one of the disciples' holsters and aimed it at Drake. Her face was red, dripping with sweat, but as determined as Kovalenko's.

"We already made a deal," Hayden said. "Honor it."

"You know nothing of honor." The Blood King spat the words. "Where was honor when you shot my father in the face?"

Dahl grunted. "You are one deluded psychopath. Just like your dad."

At a brief signal from Kovalenko, fingers tightened once more on triggers. Drake figured they were up to about three-quarters pressure.

"New deal?" Kovalenko asked. "Or dead President?"

Hayden clenched her fists and gritted her teeth before

saying anything she might regret. The tension amped up. Drake felt that, on the high grass verge, among dozens of armed men, enemies and friends, under the pitch-black skies where choppers hovered, you could hear a pin drop.

"You can't give Luther up," Mai whispered.

The disciple covering Luther didn't waver an inch. Luther stared right into the killer's eyes as if daring him to try.

"Nobody moves a muscle," the Blood King hissed, "or everyone dies."

Even Dahl was frozen in place. Drake knew they couldn't stop the murder of Coburn or Luther, let alone both. The comms were silent. Kovalenko was holding Hayden's bitter stare whilst allowing that hateful smile to hover around his lips.

"I'm gonna count to five," Luka said. "Are you ready?"

"We stick to the old deal," Hayden said. "Just go."

"No. I changed the deal. And that's 'one.'"

Mai was behind Hayden, whispering furiously. Drake knew what she was saying. Would Luka risk capture just to kill Luther?

Not a chance.

"Two."

The disciple steadied his weapon. Those covering Coburn didn't move. Luka glanced once more under the bridge.

"Three."

Molokai inched forward, desperate to save his brother. Hayden was determined to save the President. What she needed now was backup and positive actions.

"Get out of here, pal," Drake growled. "You got your shot at freedom. Don't waste it."

"And now you want me to escape," Luka laughed. "After you've hounded and chased me? After you thwarted my key plan to sell Coburn to the highest bidder? Shame on you, Matt Drake."

"Put it this way, ya fucking bell end," Alicia said. "You shoot Coburn or Luther and we shoot you. We all shoot you.

You're gonna be holier than a Tibetan monk."

The Blood King smiled grimly. "Four."

Everything fell away. There was nothing except this overloaded moment, the tension, the anticipation, the pure nerve-wracking hell of it all. Drake felt helpless and, truth be told, a little lost. Usually, they were in total control of their situation. Here, the Blood King faced overwhelming odds, and yet continued to call the shots.

It was exactly what the madman wanted.

"Five," he said.

Fingers tightened. Hayden shouted before he could finish speaking. "All right, it's a deal. Do it! Just go."

It all happened shockingly quickly. The disciples backed away, keeping Coburn in their sights. The Blood King turned and ran, darting behind them and into the shadows under the bridge. Topaz followed.

The remaining disciple shot point blank at Luther's face, but not before Hayden raised her own gun and shot him through the head. Her bullet slammed him to the right, upsetting his aim and killing him. A reflexive shot went wide of Luther, disappearing into the earth.

Mai cried out, then grabbed Hayden and stared at the still-living Luther. Her eyes were wild. Kinimaka had moved to intercept Mai but now let go. Luther himself stared down at the ground and then left and right as if shocked to be alive.

Drake and Alicia inched toward Coburn. The President lay with his back to the three disciples, painfully exposed.

Luka had vanished into the shadows. The disciples were lined up in the sights of two dozen weapons. But nobody would dare shoot, for fear of a single mistake.

The disciples backed off. Drake approached Coburn. The President looked up at him with tired, yet hopeful eyes.

"Has he escaped?"

"That remains to be seen, sir."

"It almost sounds like this is part of his plan."

"I doubt it, sir. Luka Kovalenko is a deranged madman."

Drake knelt at the President's side, still covering the slow-moving disciples. In shadow, they vanished from sight, slinking further into darkness. For one long moment, there was silence.

And then Hayden came running up. "Thank God! Oh, thank God! We have the President." She jumped on the comms. *"We have the President!"*

CHAPTER THIRTY EIGHT

For the first time since the restaurant assault back in London, Drake was able to relax a little. They had Coburn. Dozens of French troops, the police, the remaining Secret Service agent and the SPEAR team surrounded him, not to mention a dozen helicopters in the sky and several more in the fields nearby.

They fell onto the grass or sat at his side. Medics appeared, checking Coburn and everyone else that needed attention.

Drake saw next to Alicia, with Dahl on the other side. The Swede put their thoughts into words after a long moment. "It's an odd victory," he said. "Doesn't feel right."

"It's not complete," Drake said. "Kovalenko will continue to cause mayhem and hound us until he's either behind bars, or dead."

"All that shit about wanting the President to die with his family," Alicia said, "means he has even worse plans."

They took in the cool night air, enjoying the wind down.

All Drake wanted was to shrug off his armor and guns, but at that moment three American military choppers arrived, circling before landing in a nearby field. Hayden and Kinimaka drifted over.

"They're here to transport the President to the American embassy. We're all accompanying him, so make ready." Hayden had remained tight and distant ever since her decision to gamble with Luther's life. Neither the big warrior nor Mai had approached her.

"I think he has enough guards." Dahl nodded at the packed railway lines and grass verges.

"It's not just that. It's for a full debrief and threat analysis. Kovalenko's still out there. He told us he wasn't done and that his plan was foolproof."

"I suppose it's not worth reminding you 'that's what any madman would say?'" Alicia asked.

"Not at all. It's wheels up in ten."

Drake groaned as quietly as possible before pushing himself up off the muddy ground. He felt a little out of control as the next forty minutes passed with military precision. They were separated and led in groups to three different helicopters. Coburn was ushered along under a plastic cover to the first helicopter and surrounded by American soldiers.

The French watched and safeguarded the wider area. All other choppers were grounded. Drake, Alicia, Dahl, Hayden and Kinimaka were shown the next in line whilst Molokai, Luther and Mai were given the next in a nice show of diplomacy from Hayden. It took quite a feat to obtain permission for Kenzie and Dallas to accompany the President's entourage, but finally they were assigned to a fourth helicopter that was following on. Soon, they were strapped in and ready to lift off. Drake found that, even now, the tension hadn't abated. He saw it in the faces of his colleagues.

Before leaving, they received reports that there was an entrance to the underground tunnels beneath the bridge. They were still well within the environs of Paris and it was into these that Kovalenko had escaped, along with Topaz and his so-called disciples. The French had sent a team down but weren't hopeful about catching up.

As Drake waited he tilted his head back, finally able to replay some of the events of this utterly fateful night. He knew he'd never again see or speak to Lauren, Smyth and Yorgi, which made his stomach churn. Wanting company, he turned to Alicia and squeezed her hand.

"Me too," she said. "I'm gonna miss them so much."

"I want to talk about them. I want to look at old pictures. Discuss memories. I want all that."

"Me too. It doesn't feel real that I'll never get to call my little Russian friend 'Yogi' ever again. Or talk to Lauren about *Just a Touch of Nightshade.*

Drake turned his head. "Just a touch of Nightshade?"

"Her book. She was writing a book. Didn't you know?"

"Shit, no I didn't. But I wish I had."

"Well, it was probably a bit dark for you. But right up my alley."

They fell silent for a moment. Then Alicia said: "And Smyth . . ."

Their eyes teared up. Drake breathed deeply and tried to compartmentalize. Their grief wasn't for public consumption; it was barely manageable on its own.

His cell phone rang. Sighing, he pulled it out, first noticing that he'd already had three missed calls. "Bollocks," he said. "It's that +7 number again, and they've called three more times. What the fuck is happening?"

He jabbed at the answer button. This time he heard static and a faraway voice. The link was extremely weak. "Hello? *Hello?*"

Kinimaka shuffled out of his ammo belt. "Someone's got a dire need to get hold of you, brah."

"Yeah, mate, but . . . I can't hear a bloody thing."

Annoyed, he ended the call. Whoever it was would just have to ring back. "What's next for us?" he asked. "I mean, after tonight."

Hayden leaned forward. "I have a radical idea about that. Something completely different. We have no HQ. SPEAR is . . . different now anyway. We're still recovering from being disavowed and hunted only last month. I'm gonna take something to the President—when all this is over—but I need you guys to sign off on it first."

"Different?" Drake asked as the chopper took off. "Different how?"

"Let's discuss it at the embassy," Hayden said. "When we're all together."

"Not sure how Mai and Luther will feel about that," Alicia muttered.

"To be honest, I think you'll all love it. It's the best solution for everyone."

Dahl folded his arms, looking speculative. Kinimaka leant against a window, eyes closed. The chopper lifted off and rose through the air, aiming for the bright lights of central Paris. Drake allowed fatigue to seep in for a while and closed his eyes. The body needed it, but the mind couldn't rest. He was a fighter, a doer, and loyal to his friends. He couldn't relax until they were all avenged.

"Did the French get a lead on Kovalenko?" he asked, aware Hayden still had her comms system active.

"Nothing at all," came the reply. "Nothing down there. No people. No traps. No messages of any sort. He's gone."

With glittering gold lights shining in both windows, they descended into the grounds of Paris' American embassy. Coburn's helicopter was already there, rotors still chopping at the air. Drake could see a crowd of soldiers surrounding the door from which he would emerge.

"Must be a relief," he said. "For Coburn."

"Yeah, back on American soil at last," Kinimaka said.

Their machine touched the ground and cut power. Drake watched a new group of Secret Service agents surround the President. It was a bittersweet moment. Kinimaka unlocked the door and they took their time climbing out.

The air was cold, biting. The skies were clear, the stars shimmering and strewn from horizon to horizon. Drake turned when an excited shout rang out. He was surprised to see the President's children come running down the embassy steps, straight toward their father. Coburn took a long moment to hug them and then looked up.

"How are you here? And where's your mom?"

One of the new Secret Service agents appeared right behind the children. "She's right here, sir. The bullet missed her vital organs and she's stable. The journey from London to Paris is so short, and with the hospital already being compromised, we thought it best to vacate it and bring everyone to the embassy here in Paris."

"Is that wise? Stable or not, it's a risk."

"Not at all, sir. Not with the facilities and medics we have aboard Air Force One. And, well . . . your wife did insist. The doctors signed off. They wanted to be here for you."

Coburn turned to the children. "That sounds like your mum. How is she?"

"She says she's feeling much better now and wants to see you."

"Lead the way."

Coburn threw Hayden and the SPEAR team a last glance as he was guided toward the embassy doors. Several medics appeared and tried persuading him to stop for attention, but he informed them that first, he would visit his wife.

"We have no HQ?" Kinimaka suddenly said out of the blue. "I didn't know that."

Hayden smiled and walked inside. Drake followed. Time passed as they were shown to a buffet room. They took food and water, allowing their bodies to replenish its depleted reserves. Kenzie and Dallas joined them, complaining about red tape and annoying searches.

Alicia enjoyed a few moments quizzing Kenzie as to the appropriateness of it all. Hayden again voiced her commitment to explaining her new proposition—including Kenzie in her comment—and Dahl mentioned the fact that they really should find Kovalenko first.

"But he might vanish for months," Hayden said. "He was fond of saying this plan took years of preparation. Why wouldn't the next?"

"You could be retired by then." Dahl grinned at Drake.

"Hey—"

"That's partly the plan," Hayden added.

Drake tried to hold his glare at the Swede but couldn't. A second trip to the buffet beckoned and the ice water was already helping to reinvigorate his body. Alicia was already looking from him to one of the exit doors.

"I wonder where the bedrooms are?"

"I doubt they'll just give us a bedroom, Alicia." Drake grabbed a handful of salt and vinegar crisps.

"Well, a spare bathroom cubicle then."

Drake checked his watch. It had been a little over two hours since they lifted off. The SPEAR team was assembled, looking casual, refreshed, and—

He blinked rapidly and then looked again before shouting at everyone to be quiet.

"What the hell? Where are Mai, Luther and Molokai?"

CHAPTER THIRTY NINE

Mai settled in as their chopper lifted off. It was the last in line, which was good. It wasn't a long journey to the embassy and she wanted to clear her mind for a short while. It had been a long time since she'd felt serious feelings for a man— and that man had been Matt Drake. She wasn't there yet with Luther but she saw a chance. She felt it. Beneath all the swagger and the blunt force, she knew Luther was a decent man. He had heart. He felt loyalty. He was compassionate, respectful and funny. Tender even.

Of course, he hid it well. But peel away the layers and there was a good man.

Mai fought through tears for her friends that had died, worry for her family in Tokyo that were still in hiding, and the fact that she'd been forced to risk the President's life for Luther's. And how did she feel about Hayden now that they had time to reflect?

It had been one of the riskiest calls Mai had ever seen, and she had witnessed many. Hayden had taken the burden upon herself alone, and would have accepted the consequences. It showed leadership. It proved Team SPEAR followed the right person. But if Hayden had missed?

What then?

Mai stared at Luther, who sat opposite. The large man had been quiet since the event. "She made the right call. Don't punish her for it," he said.

"You wouldn't be saying that if you were dead, boy," Molokai grumped from the far side.

"Stop being a big brother for one minute. And you—" he indicated Mai "—stop regretting you missed your chance at this after our date night." He indicated his body. "Put yourself in Hayden's shoes. She chose correctly."

Mai made a face. "I see that now, asshole."

They fell into silence. The chopper banked after the others. They'd departed five minutes later so couldn't see those ahead. Paris glittered below, the same city of extremes as it had been throughout time. The chopper veered once more and then picked up speed, heading for the center. Mai took a moment to assess Luther.

"But what happens next?" she asked. "Kovalenko is missing. He killed our friends. Team SPEAR is without a home. We never have any personal time to speak of. No life other than being soldiers. So . . . what's next?"

"Is this a test? Sounds like it to me."

"Maybe."

"Stick together," Luther said, "with work. Live apart, in life. And please, you guys have to take a fucking break from all this."

Mai almost smiled. The advice was sound but putting it into practice wasn't going to be easy. Perhaps they could work something out once they were through this. Of course, nothing would ever be the same.

"What I want now—" she turned to Molokai "—is to hear a little bit more about the mysterious man on our team. I'm sure you have a radical story, my friend. Where does it begin?"

Molokai pursed his lips. "I admit I wasn't ready for the question. You want me to distract you, don't you? Well, I guess I could—"

The chopper dropped thirty feet. Mai felt her stomach slam up into her mouth, and grabbed one of the safety straps. The pilot shouted, pulling on the collective and reaching for the radio.

Bullets strafed the chopper. They were so low that the tops of tall structures practically scraped paint off their underside. The pilot swerved around a spire, and barely missed crashing into the top floor of a hotel. Glaring rows of lights flashed by.

Mai, Luther and Molokai held on as the pilot yelled out a

warning. He'd seen a helipad ahead on top of one of the luxury hotels and was going to try to land. Mai watched through the nearest window. Another bright tracery of gunfire arched toward them. Several shots hit. The chopper shuddered. Its engine took on an unfamiliar whine.

The pilot turned. "Hydraulics are hit. That's gonna affect our flight ability."

"Crap," Luther said. "Not what we wanna hear a hundred feet in the air."

"We have to climb." The pilot finessed his controls and took the chopper higher. The luxury hotel was dead ahead. Another volley of bullets smashed into the engine bay. The pilot let out a string of curses.

"Fuck it," he said. "I'm landing this thing in the street."

The chopper nose-dived. Mai clung on, trying to remain calm. This was out of her control. Molokai was looking to get a bead on the bullets. Luther clung to a strap and smiled, rocking with the chopper's movements, giving the impression that he was riding out a fairground simulator.

They dipped toward a busy road, leveled and then glided forward with the nose up. Vehicles skidded out of the way below them. Streetlights flashed by dangerously close to both sides. Mai readied her weapons. A gap opened in the traffic ahead, and the pilot took full advantage, dropping the chopper onto the asphalt. The skids hit at an awkward angle. Mai was thrown to the left, smashing her temple on the bulkhead. A heavy grating sound drowned out everything else, even the tortured whine of the engine. Finally, the skids buckled, the chopper dropped further, and its bulk hit the road.

Oncoming vehicles slewed in all directions, lights blinding as they tried to avoid the helicopter.

Mai shook herself, trying to clear a murky head. The blow to her temple had disorientated her. Luther reached over, unbuckled her belt, and moved to the door. Molokai opened the other side and the pilot checked the controls, shutting the machine down.

"C'mon." Luther dragged her out into the street. The cold air bit clean through her haze. She put a hand to her temple, felt blood, and raised her weapon.

"This doesn't make any sense," she mumbled. "We were the third chopper. We were—"

The pilot came around the front of his machine, gun drawn. He aimed it at Luther first. "Chosen," he finished the sentence for her. "You were chosen."

He fired. Mai saw a thick black dart appear in Luther's neck. An instant later his legs buckled, and he fell to his knees. Mai had already lined the pilot up for a kill shot but for some reason he was still smiling.

"Put down here on purpose," he said. "Chopper's fine."

There was a stinging sensation in the back of her neck and then a feeling of numbness flooding through her veins, saturating her system. She fired her gun, but she was already falling. The bullet glanced off the road. The gun fell from nerveless fingers. She remained aware; she could see everything that was happening.

But she was paralyzed.

Collapsing next to Luther, she stared into his eyes and saw the barest twitch. They'd been tagged with some kind of drug. She could hear everything quite clearly. The fall of Molokai, the approach of at least four men, the congratulations they gave to the pilot.

"Went without a hitch," one said. "Luka will reward you."

"We should get out of here now," another said. "People are watching. Recording this on cell phones."

"Let them watch," laughed the first voice. "The legendary warriors Luther and Mai Kitano are about to be shipped to Devil's Island. I don't see them ever coming back."

"What about the other one?"

"Don't need anyone else. Shoot him."

"I'm shooting nobody in front of all these people. They have our faces on their cell phones, as you said."

"All right, all right. Leave him. Just load them up fast. Now."

Mai felt her body lifted, hands supporting her. She landed heavily on a van floor but felt nothing. Luther crashed down beside her. No matter how hard she tried she couldn't reach for him, couldn't touch him.

She breathed, and that was all.

Devil's Island?

Time passed, she knew not how much. Eventually their transport stopped, and the back doors swung open. More words were passed. She and Luther were dragged out into the cold night air and carried for about two dozen steps. Then she heard steel grating—a metal door opening and crashing back into more metal.

"Stand back!" one of her captors shouted. "Stand back or we'll taze you so hard you'll shake for a week."

Mai was carried over a threshold into a dim, unwavering light. The walls and roof of this new place were steel and corrugated. The floor was echoey, also made of steel. As they carried her along its length, she understood she was being taken into a shipping container.

They let her fall hard onto the floor. She felt nothing. She caught a glimpse of Luther's large body landing at her side.

"Take care of them," the voice told somebody she hadn't yet seen. "They'll be joining you in your new home."

Laughter followed. Footsteps walked to the exit and then a door clanged shut.

Mai stared helplessly at a rusted metal ceiling.

And then a single word jolted her memory.

"Mai?"

A face hovered over her, staring down. The eyes were wide, full of concern and fear, but Mai recognized them.

What on earth is Karin Blake doing here?

CHAPTER FORTY

Drake sat calmly, waiting for Hayden to return. He was worried about Mai and the others, but Hayden had rushed to the embassy's communications room to find out what was happening.

"Don't worry, she'll turn up," Alicia told him. "She's probably just bouncing around on Luther's—"

"We should review everything Kovalenko told us," Drake interrupted. "His plans, his threats, his ideas even. Karin hasn't turned up, so we have to assume what we heard about her being taken to Devil's Island is true."

"I can check for anything related to that," Kinimaka said and picked up a laptop.

"I hate knowing Kovalenko's still out there," Kenzie said. "Just plotting our deaths. And Topaz? Me and that girl will have a reckoning."

Dallas sat beside her. "She got lucky."

"Yeah, damn right she did. But it was my own fault. I thought I had her, got smug. I didn't see you helping although."

"Still waiting, girl." Dallas rubbed his thumb and forefinger together.

Dahl winced, staring at Kenzie. "Are you going to let him get away with that?"

Kenzie sighed. "It's not derogatory. It's just Dallas."

"Is that a new tagline? And where did you meet?"

Kenzie stared. "What the fuck does it have to do with you? Suddenly, you care? You want me back? I gave you the chance. I won't be stupid enough to do that again."

"That's not what I—"

"Save it. Now look, when can I get the fuck out of here?"

Dallas was watching them both with interest. "I see there's history here."

"Yeah, and if you know what's good for you, stay out of it," Kenzie snapped.

Kinimaka looked up from the laptop he was pecking away at. "Maybe after Hayden delivers her proposition you could leave if you still want to. Don't you wanna hear it?"

"Not sure that I care."

Hayden came around the corner at that point. "Bad news," she said. "Molokai just called. He could barely speak. Says Mai and Luther were taken after their chopper came under fire. The pilot was working for Kovalenko."

Drake shot to his feet. "Where?"

"I don't know, but this embassy was also just put on high alert."

"Here? Why?" Dahl looked shocked.

"Because Kovalenko's not done," Drake said. "He told us that."

"Where's the President?" Alicia asked.

"With his family."

"He told us that too. The President would die with his family."

"You can't seriously believe he's going to hit the US embassy?" Dahl walked over to a window.

"Judging by all that he's done so far, and all his father did," Drake said. "I'd say it's a given."

"Now?" Kinimaka asked.

"Now."

CHAPTER FORTY ONE

Luka Kovalenko watched the Parisian US embassy, a satisfied sneer on his harsh face. He'd escaped the combined might of SPEAR, the French and American military back there without a single scratch. And not once had his final plan for the President been put in jeopardy. Everything had led to this.

Now came the real risk with the big payoff. The second part of his long vengeance. The first had been taking out various members of the SPEAR team. The third wasn't far away.

Karin and her friend, Mai and Luther, were safely packed away, ready to set sail to the Pacific. Nobody would find them until the Blood King allowed it.

Luka was aware that he'd come a long way. Why risk it all now? First, from the son of a revered, enigmatic oligarch to a stray rat crawling the streets. It would have been so much easier to give up, to join the mewling wannabees and has-beens, to lose his identity among the masses. What life would he have carved out then? Maybe a good one.

Or maybe I'd already be dead.

He regretted the loss of Andrei. His father's enforcer had proven helpful in joining the fractured gangs together, in furthering all Luka's plans. Still, there was always another Andrei.

Topaz lay at his side, using another pair of field glasses to evaluate the embassy. An army was gathered at their backs.

Turning now, he sent the men on their way. Soon they would be in position.

Luka put his field glasses down for a moment and turned to the seven-inch monitor at his right hand. Its screen showed a blueprint of the embassy itself. Almost at the very center of that blueprint was a small, white blip.

"Coburn hasn't moved for some time," he said. "He must be with his family."

"Agreed," Topaz said, shifting.

"Are you ready to go to work?"

"You know that I am."

Luka reached out and placed a fond hand on her shoulder. "We'll see each other again," he said. "Tomorrow."

"Of course, Luka. But do you really need this? Now?"

He knew what she meant. Already, he'd done enough to take the mantle of the Blood King. To wear it with pride. Nobody could take that away from him or challenge it. But he sensed a small wavering on Topaz's part, a willingness to move on, and reached out to where she would feel it the most.

"Don't you want what I want, my love?" His eyes met hers.

As he'd expected, she looked away. "You know that I do."

"Then do as I ask and tear that building apart."

She rolled away and left him alone, taking her place with his soldiers. Luka concentrated on the small white blip that was the President of the United States and sneered. *I see you. I'm coming for you.* Hours ago, he had offered Coburn bottled water. Within the miniscule electrolytes had been a very advanced form of tracker, the kind America's own CIA used to keep tabs on people all over the world. It would last for days, possibly weeks as it saturated Coburn's system.

America had the brains, the resources and the power to rule the world with ease. It was the people their own government, its CIA and greedy politicians, sold those ideas to for immense profit that caused the problem. Luka studied the building and its grounds once more, then reviewed the plan in his head.

They'll never know what hit them.

He was ready to lead the attack. He was ready to prove that he was the real Blood King. Nothing had ever meant more to him than this perfect moment.

This is me, Luka Kovalenko, and I will become my father. I am his legacy.

He sat upright and inspected his weapons. Next, he checked the comms. Finally, he confirmed his army was ready.

Could a moment be any more perfect?

The Blood King attacked.

CHAPTER FORTY TWO

"You hear that?" Drake asked. "What the hell is that?"

They listened. Dahl was at the window. Drake joined him. "See anything out there, mate?"

"Quiet as the grave."

Drake looked over a courtyard leading to a black wrought iron fence topped with gold filigree. He hoped it was stronger than it looked. Iron gates of the same style as the fence stood at the center, backed up by a single guard tower. Drake saw US Marines outside, backing up the guards. The Secret Service had been warned.

"I don't see how we're in danger here," Dallas said. "We're inside the—"

"Stop right there, newbie," Alicia said. "You didn't fight the last Blood King."

"The *last* Blood King? What are they? Clones?"

The odd sound came again, a whining, resounding thunder. Drake strained his eyes. The courtyard was well lit, but the area beyond sat in pools of dark and the buildings across the way were unlit at this time of night. Try as he might he couldn't discern a source for the noise.

"Hope the guards can see over there," Dahl said, squinting. " 'Cause I can't see shit."

If an attack was coming it would happen quickly. Kovalenko wouldn't risk the President and his family reaching safety again. The heavy whining noise came again. A stray, dreadful thought struck him, and it was then that he knew what was about to happen. It was right then that he caught on.

"Oh fuck," he said. "Hang on. Get ready to brace!"

At the same time he hit the comms button. "Marines! Clear that front door."

Dahl made a perplexed gesture, but then everyone at the

window saw it coming. A predator dressed in darkness coming out of the pitch black.

Hayden made it out and gasped. "A helicopter? But they grounded the flights. All of them."

"But it was already here." Drake hissed. "That clever bastard. It's the chopper they crash-landed earlier, just a few blocks away. He always planned to use it this way."

The SPEAR team backed away as the chopper flew in. There was no deviance in its flight, no margin for error. It rose over the surrounding buildings and dove for the American embassy. Drake picked out its broken skids and dented hull in the meager light and knew he was right.

"Move."

It flew at a sharp downward angle. The marines opened fire, bullets spraying the cockpit and fuselage. But then a streak of white fire shot toward them.

"No," Dahl muttered, frozen at the window.

The rocket propelled grenade struck one of the gate's supports, shattering it to pieces. Two more streaks followed, destroying the fence and the guard tower. Alicia jumped on the Swede, grabbing him by the shoulders and pulling him to the ground.

"Duck, Torsty, duck. I mean, what the fuck?"

Drake heard the chopper's last moments as it flew over the top of the collapsing fence and smashed straight into the American embassy. The impact was dreadful. The whole building shook, making mortar fall from the walls and ceiling. A ball of fire swept up from the impact, shattering windows and temporarily lighting their room in hellish orange.

Alicia felt shards strike her back. Dahl brushed them off.

Drake leapt from his knees to his feet. "On me."

Together, they exited the room and headed for the stairs. The embassy was in uproar. Hayden pulled out a small tablet monitor and checked on the President's position. "He's still in the family quarters."

Drake made a quick decision. Keep going. They were blind to events out front. Maybe they could curtail the attack right by the doors. They reached a balcony and looked over, seeing the devastation below. Helicopter parts were scattered, smoldering, across the front lobby. Part of the wall had collapsed. Drake saw men and women down, injured and dead. Marines were on their knees, tending to the wounded amid the rubble.

"Look out!" he cried.

Through the front first-floor window he saw more rockets inbound and, in the glow they shed as they approached the embassy, a force of men. Two explosions splintered his senses. More wall collapsed. Debris detonated in all directions as Drake hit the floor.

"It's a fucking war zone," Dallas cried.

It soon will be, Drake thought and lifted his head to raw battle.

Gunfire sounded from outside, loud above the blazing wreckage and groans of the injured. Drake saw their balcony had been half torn away and was hanging over the sheer drop to the lobby floor. He heard it creak as he crawled to the edge, looking down.

Mercenaries poured into the embassy. They wore helmets and full body armor and were well armed. Without pause, Drake fired down at them. Bullets struck and sent them reeling, but the sheer mass of them allowed many to pass below, out of his line of sight. Dahl and Alicia joined him at the edge, firing down.

Their joint fire sent half a dozen men flying, many groaning as their armor took the full brunt of the shot. Drake concentrated his firepower on the holes in the wall where the majority were climbing in.

Some fell. Others leapt sideways. Several tripped over their colleagues and large lumps of rubble.

"I'm counting dozens," Dahl said. "We're talking over a hundred if they keep coming like this."

Hayden was on the comms, guarded by Kinimaka. "Breach at the front," she said. "Is Eagle at the bunker?"

"Heading there now."

Drake looked back. "Where's the bunker?"

Hayden closed her eyes in fear. "Put it this way. The mercs are headed in the right direction."

"We can't get down there fast enough!" Alicia cried.

Drake spied the staircase at the far end of their corridor. It was over a hundred feet away. "Shit, you're right."

"Are you kidding?" Dahl was already in motion. "Man up, you fucking pussies."

He leapt out over the drop, grabbed hold of the broken, hanging handrail, and let his weight pull it toward the floor below. It creaked, cracked and lowered gently at first. Drake saw his chance and jumped on too. Alicia came third and that was when the wooden structure fell. Dahl landed feet first among the slain enemy. Drake fell onto his side and rolled, shrugging it off. Alicia hit the shoulders of a running merc. The two collapsed in a messy jumble.

Drake yanked her to her feet, shooting the merc through the head. All of a sudden they were in the midst of battle, at the center of running men. Hayden and the others would have to find their own way. Drake saw dozens of mercs and several marines battling just outside, on the embassy steps. He saw helmeted enemies all around. He ducked and fired, killing three. A barrel slammed into his gut; the impact absorbed by his own armor but still unbalancing him. He staggered, tripping another man. Dahl was ahead, shooting and trying to fight through the surge. The corridor that led from the lobby to the back of the house was almost completely blocked by men.

Luckily, Drake had access to the comms. "I see meeting rooms back there. A ballroom. I see kitchens."

Hayden came back: "The President had to turn back. I think the initial attack, the flow of enemy, is designed to cut off access to the bunker."

"Then we're in real trouble."

"Luckily, it's a big embassy. He can hide."

Drake had memorized the embassy's general layout. He knew where the President was headed. The second most defensible place in the whole house. He explained to Dahl and Alicia through the comms and, as one, they cut to the right, pounding through a high-ceilinged ballroom.

There were more mercs ahead, communicating through comms of their own. Was it possible that they knew where Coburn was? As he ran he relayed the thought to Hayden.

"I'll pass it along," Hayden replied. "That'll change everything. How far away are you?"

"Not far."

They came up behind a trio of mercs and dispatched them without mercy. A narrow corridor lay ahead, wooden paneling broken up by bronze sconces and gold-framed paintings. Every decoration had a French touch. No doubt a gentle reminder of whose country they were in. At the end of the corridor, a staircase wound up to higher floors.

Dahl hit the steps two at a time. Alicia followed. Drake brought up the rear. For now, they were alone, pounding through a quiet section of the house. Distant gunfire erupted and there was the sound of something collapsing.

Dahl gained the next floor and slowed, checking ahead.

"We're clear."

"Third floor," Drake said. "The President's family room. After the bunker, it's the only other defensible area in the house."

"Makes sense, since that's where he'll spend a great deal of time."

They climbed. Through the comms they heard Hayden approaching from the east. They radioed the Secret Service to expect them and were met with gratitude.

"And the mercs?" Kenzie asked.

Drake glanced down the stairs. "Right behind us."

CHAPTER FORTY THREE

The SPEAR team regrouped in the corridor and approached the President's room at a sprint. The Secret Service agents were ready, along with several marines, opening the doors just as Hayden reached them.

"How long do we have?" an agent asked.

"Twenty seconds," Drake said. "Prepare yourselves."

He took in the entire room. It was a large, square area with a double bed to the right, away from the window. A door at the far end led to a bathroom.

"It's a mini safe-room," a marine told him. "Eagle and his family are inside, protected by six men."

It was a small saving grace, Drake knew, that the children and Marie wouldn't see what was about to happen.

In the next second he recognized the snarl from outside the locked door. "Bring me their heads."

Luka Kovalenko.

"It's on," he said.

Bullets stitched holes through the door and walls. Drake took cover behind an assortment of dressers, a mattress, a layer of spare bullet-proof vests and, he thought, the nice added touch of several French paintings, which bore the brunt of the attack.

The door was pounded again and again; boots, bodies and weapons smashing at the heavy timbers. He joined the Secret Service in returning fire, giving those outside no quarter. They would have to go through sheer hell to get in here, every step gained through blood and torture.

The door splintered. A hole appeared in the wall. Grenades blasted even more of it apart. Huge chunks of breeze block fell into the room. A volley of bullets sent the defenders to the ground, ducking behind their makeshift barrier, and a surge of attackers poured through.

Drake was up to meet them. He turned the HK in his hands to smash a man point blank in the face, then used the swing to strike another across the temple. Several men crashed into their barricade, disturbing it. Jackets and paintings slithered to the floor.

Dahl grabbed a man under the arms and pulled him over the barricade, over his shoulder, and slammed him to the ground. He threw a drawer at another's mouth whilst shooting a third. The enemy kept coming like an unstoppable flood.

The defenders were forced back halfway to the bathroom. Kenzie and Dallas fought at each other's side, the latter looking shell-shocked as he fought off two attackers whilst ignoring a knife wound across the left bicep. Hayden and Kinimaka bobbed and weaved at the back of the pack, sighting enemies with their Glocks and taking them down, attempting to stem the flow through the shattered wall.

Alicia hit low, darting around the barricade and shooting out knees, shins and thighs. This was not the time for mercy. This was a pitiless terrorist attack against the President, his family, and the civilized world.

The defenders held them off for a while, even started to inch forward, but then Luka appeared through the door, Topaz at his side. Crazed with blood lust, the Blood King shouted for grenades.

And they were launched.

Three flew high, over the defenders' heads, and hit the back wall, rebounding off the bathroom door. Drake, his colleagues, agents and marines dived across the collapsing barricade to take cover.

Some of the enemy didn't see what was happening and were caught as all three grenades exploded at once. The explosive blast tore them apart, wounded others and buckled the bathroom wall. Plaster exploded to reveal thick chunks of bullet-resistant fiberglass, the bare shell of the safe room.

Luka ran forward, covered by Topaz. Drake saw an opportunity.

So did Kenzie.

Crying out, the Israeli climbed the collapsing barricade and used it to launch herself at the scarred Russian assassin. The two collapsed in a heap.

Drake threw an opponent aside to confront Luka. "Where are Mai and Luther?"

"Safe for now. They're with Karin Blake and her soldier friend."

"What is Devil's Island?"

Luka grinned amidst the battle. "The greatest, most beautiful, most deadly place on earth. Your friends will love it."

Laughing, the Blood King attacked Drake. He was fast, brutal, and trained. Drake didn't underestimate him. To the right, Topaz and Kenzie were engaged in a ferocious tangle of hand-to-hand combat, both ducking and diving, rolling and rising, and striking with deadly blows. Blood spilled. They cried out as they struck each other, whether with the force of the blow or wounds Drake didn't know.

A marine fell to his left, the last of them. Another Secret Service agent was shot. His own team struggled to hold on and were not without injuries. Dallas was bleeding from the head, down on one knee and barely able to defend himself.

Kinimaka was on his back, fighting two men, one arm locked to the ground by a third. Hayden was backed up against the safe room itself, fighting to her last breath for President Coburn, two Secret Service agents at her side. Drake saw her shoot one of Mano's attackers and take a blow to the ribs that bent her double.

Two bullets struck Alicia, making her cry out and backpedal at speed into one of the broken windows. Whatever glass remained shattered around her and she fell to the ground, eyes alive with pain and regret.

The enemy kept coming.

Drake forced Luka back, drawing blood from the man's nose. He saw Kenzie rolling on top of Topaz, battering the assassin's face until it turned red, but then Topaz got lucky. Her grasping fingers found an edge of broken picture frame, grabbed it, and drove it into the side of Kenzie's head.

The Israeli fell away, not even screaming. The frame stuck up out of her skull, drawing Drake's attention. *Oh no.*

Topaz struggled to her knees, wiping blood from her face. She raised a boot over the frame shard, ready to drive it through Kenzie's brain.

Dahl hit her full force, sending her tumbling, breaking her right shoulder in the process. Topaz screamed as she came to a stop against the wall. Dahl sprawled to her right, having forgone all thoughts of defense in the attack. All he wanted to do was save Kenzie. Now he lay amid enemy soldiers, without backup, alone and vulnerable.

Topaz clutched her shoulder. A boot smashed down on Dahl's spine. Drake sought to fend off Luka and rush to the Swede's aid, but the Blood King held him back. Alicia was still out of it, gasping for breath and trying to find her feet. Everyone else was down.

Drake saw that the end had come.

The safe room was being torn down, blasts having weakened the struts and kick plates. There was a gap through which its inhabitants could be seen. More paneling was being ripped off. Inside, six agents and two marines formed a final ring around the President and his family, a last stand.

Hayden and Kinimaka were crawling through to join it.

Dahl groaned in agony. Topaz held her knife above his spine and plunged it downward. Drake saw a blur.

Kenzie.

Still with the shard sticking out of her skull, she threw herself at Topaz, kicked the woman in the head and then leaped up, straight at the wall. For a second Drake thought she had gone crazy, but then she hit one of the displays up there, shattering the outer glass and letting it fall to the floor where it broke apart.

Two French swords gifted to President Coburn. Two *brand new* French swords.

Kenzie ignored the shard, picked up a sword and swept it at Topaz's head. The woman reeled away, raising her knife and deflecting the blade. She fell to the side. Kenzie struck again, her flashing blade coming down hard.

Topaz swiped at it with the knife, and managed to propel it aside once more. The sound of clashing steel resounded around the room. The knife flew away. Kenzie stood over Topaz with her sword raised. "Die hard, bitch."

The swipe of the blade removed Topaz's head from her shoulders.

Luka had been watching, and sagged, his eyes going wide.

Drake saw Dahl roll to Kenzie's feet and the woman raise her sword, ready to protect him as three mercs prepared to attack.

Seeing Kenzie, they paused.

Drake ignored Luka, raised his gun and fired. He took four mercenaries out in seconds. Alicia, by the window, had recovered enough to read the situation and did the same. Kenzie thrust her sword through another's chest.

Drake kicked the Blood King away, and this time fired the gun at him. Exhaustion made the bullet fly low, striking the chest plate instead of the neck, where he'd been aiming.

Luka fell back, stunned.

Drake turned and emptied the rest of his mag into those mercs assaulting the safe room. Three fell, dead. The remaining four spun in anger.

Hayden and Kinimaka rose up in their midst. The big Hawaiian used a large knife, slitting throats. Hayden used her Glock at close range, taking the rest down.

Luka looked very much alone.

But he still had twenty men at his back.

The SPEAR team attacked as one, the last defenders of the President of the United States. They were fighting for their murdered friends—for Yorgi, Lauren and Smyth. For others they didn't know but honored. For Coburn's wife and children. They were the bloodied last line, and they were determined to save everything that remained, everything they loved and respected.

Mercs hesitated in the face of all that fury. They staggered under bullet impacts, under the blows of swords and fists. They fell, dead and dying. They retreated hard, dragging a screaming Luka Kovalenko with them.

"I won't leave her. I want Topaz!"

Under a fresh onslaught, the mercs retreated. Drake expected a covering burst of fire and got it. The mercs hurled grenades and ran. He took cover along with everyone else.

A minute later came more grenades, and then after another minute: more. Drake expected Luka to have positioned men all the way back to the gate to facilitate an escape.

He couldn't give chase. Instead, he looked to his friends and then to President Coburn. "Are we all good?"

"Battered to shit," Alicia said. "But generally . . . I think so."

Agents were crawling through the dust. The President rose among them, a revolver in hand, his kids tucked behind him, his wife still in bed and attached to wires at the back of the room. Drake forced down a rush of emotion on seeing that sight. That picture alone was worthy of a presidency.

"Do we have anything left?" he asked. "The energy to go after Kovalenko?"

Dahl dragged his body up off the floor, grimacing. "I do."

Kenzie clashed her swords together. "Let's go."

Judging by the sounds, Drake guessed the mercenaries were heading downstairs. With the noise of battle dissipated he could hear sirens in the streets, men shouting and the thunder of helicopters.

"One more fight."

CHAPTER FORTY FOUR

The SPEAR team came together, ready to give chase. Kovalenko couldn't be allowed to breathe fresh air in this world. Not anymore. Not after this.

Drake walked through the damaged doorway, reloading as he went. Dahl followed and then came Alicia. Kenzie helped Dallas up. The guy walked with a heavy limp, but was game to continue. It was only as they moved out that they heard Hayden's voice.

"Wait!"

Drake paused. *Now what?*

She walked into the corridor, holding her ribs and breathing hard. "We're the last line of defense," she said. "If we go after Kovalenko now, the President has only five Secret Service agents to guard him."

Drake hesitated, drawn to help Coburn but aware that if they let Kovalenko escape, his return would be inevitable.

"The bastard took Mai. Luther. Karin. If we let him go he'll strike again."

"Take the victory now," Hayden said, "and return to the battle tomorrow. C'mon, guys. Coburn's kids are here too."

Drake didn't hesitate, just walked back into the room with Dahl at his side. Together, they assessed the situation. "Are you ready to move out?"

"Yes, sir," an agent said. "Locked and loaded. Air Force One came from London with your family and is warming as we speak."

"Then let's get the fuck out of here."

With free access to the bunker, they moved in a group down the stairs. Never stopping, they kept the First Family at the center and circled them, guns up and prepared to open fire.

They skirted fire, rubble and dead bodies. The bunker

came up quickly and was locked at their backs, offering an unbreachable guard, but they didn't stop. The President had been checked for nano-trackers and now Drake watched as the Secret Service agents prepared a formula in the bunker that would negate them, courtesy of a phone call to the CIA. Minutes later, they were exiting the bunker, this time by a different door.

Tunnels took them through three more heavy reinforced doors and past a small armory. Everyone took the time to replenish their weapons and ammo reserves, and also to replace damaged body armor. Soon, they were on their way again, following the rough-hewn path until it rose toward a door.

An agent paused by a keypad. "Eagle is on site." He dipped his head as he spoke.

"Ready to go," a voice answered in Drake's ear.

The agent hit a code then exited with caution, backed up by his colleagues. Drake exited into the pitch-black, pre-dawn darkness, sniffing the cold, fresh air.

Before them, rumbling loudly, stood one of the most welcome sights of the last twenty four hours.

Air Force One.

"This isn't Charles de Gaulle," Dahl looked around.

"It's an emergency runway," the marine replied, "reserved for times of war. We and the French figured this qualified."

"I think they want me out of their country." President Coburn gave a tight smile. "And back to my own."

"Well, let's go then." Hayden led the way out of the tunnel and across the tarmac. Two lines of soldiers awaited them, forming a cordon all the way to the lowered aircraft door.

Drake scanned the skies as he ran. He wouldn't put anything past the Blood King. If a single one of these soldiers had been turned, or coerced . . .

On a hair-trigger the SPEAR team ran alongside the President. It didn't take long. Soon, they were climbing the steps and entering the aircraft, finding seats. The First

Family were whisked away. Before everyone had buckled in, the aircraft moved. In another few minutes it was roaring down the runway.

Straight into a hard, almost vertical take-off.

Drake gripped the seat handles. It was a necessary vigorous climb, but by the time the plane leveled off, Drake was looking at his teammates with something like surreal disbelief in his eyes.

After all that, they were headed back to DC, leaving the chaos behind. Apart from the roar of the engines, there was total silence.

Drake breathed a sigh of relief.

CHAPTER FORTY FIVE

Battered, lost and overwhelmed with heartache, Drake and his friends settled in for their long flight aboard Air Force One.

Hayden spoke to Cambridge in London and a new contact back in Paris before furnishing them with more information.

"Lauren and Smyth are being flown to DC," she said. "For burial. I think they would have wanted to stay close."

Drake nodded, unable to speak for a moment. "There's something else," he said after a pause. "Yorgi's wish was to relocate the graves of his brothers and sister. We must do that and maybe put them beside him. Somewhere warm and sunny. That's his closure."

"Agreed," Hayden inclined her head for a few moments before continuing. "Wholeheartedly. But first, there is the ongoing issue before us. Kovalenko escaped. Whereabouts unknown. It is certain that he has further plans. Everyone must remain vigilant. London is on lockdown. Paris too. Every major city in the world is at its highest alert."

"Is this a good time for your proposal?" Kinimaka asked, leaning so far forward his seat groaned beneath him.

"No, Mano. That proposal is for the whole SPEAR team. Not part of it."

Dahl nodded in agreement. "Which leads us to the bigger issue at hand. What happened to Karin, Mai and Luther?"

"They're alive and on their way to Devil's Island," Drake recalled Kovalenko's words. "He wanted us to know that."

"Which means he wants us there too," Alicia said.

"Happy to oblige," Dahl said. "Not that I don't have faith in our friends' skills to survive and escape, but I'd like to help them do it."

"And bury the Blood King on that island," Drake said. "Once and for all."

Kenzie leaned forward, upsetting Dallas who was trying to wrap a bandage around her head wound. "I know I quit the team," she said. "But that was before Kovalenko. He attacked me too. And I'd like to help you."

"Girl," Alicia said, mimicking Dallas. "We'd be happy to have you."

Kenzie narrowed her eyes in mock anger. "Careful."

Dallas fought to fasten the bandage with a safety pin. "Hold still will you. I can't quite get it in."

Alicia laughed. "You sound like Drake in bed after a pint of shandy."

Drake ignored the comment. "Any clues on Kovalenko? Direction? Snitch feedback? Military intelligence?"

"Not so far, but they'll be working it around the clock until the day he's found."

"Which brings us back to Devil's Island."

Kinimaka sighed. "I found no references to it in the short time that I sniffed around the Internet," he said. "But I do wonder if there might be some mention on the Dark Web. We are dealing with criminal masterminds and underworld kingpins, after all."

Drake paused, aware that it had been a long time since the team had shared a post-mission discussion with some of their number missing, and some of their number dead. It was disturbing and heart-breaking at the same time, charged with emotion.

President Coburn appeared down the aisle. He came with two guards but asked them to stay behind as he approached. He stopped next to Hayden.

"Once again you have helped save my life," he addressed the team. "And the lives of my family. I can't thank you enough. If you ever need anything, just ask."

Drake held his eyes, smiling. "I saw you, sir, ready to die to save your children. That sight was more than enough thanks for me."

Coburn inclined his head, eyes a little teary. Drake

expected Hayden to thank the man and move on with their discussion, but instead she asked him a question. "Sir, I have a proposal. I'm not able to speak about it until we're reunited with the rest of our team, but I'd like the opportunity at a later date."

Coburn nodded. "Miss Jaye. People," he spread his arms to include all of them, "if it's within my power to give you what you want, it's yours."

He moved away, smiling once more. In the silence that followed, Drake's cell phone rang. Still smiling, still deflecting the grief he wanted to vent, he fished it out and checked the screen.

"The +7 number again." He shook his head. "I'm gonna reject it for now."

"No." Dahl reached out. "It might be important."

Drake leaned back, hitting the speakerphone. "Hello?"

This time the line crackled, a distant voice spoke, but he couldn't make out any of it. Everyone else frowned. Drake shook the phone irritably. "Can't hear you, mate. Hello?"

For just a moment, an utterly flawless signal found the connection and a distinct voice boomed over the line.

"It's me. It's Yorgi. They thought I was dead, but I wasn't. I've been trying to contact you for ages. Where the hell have you been?"

Drake couldn't describe the incredible sense of utter shock, happiness and disbelief that consumed him in that moment. It was like being doused in a bucket of ice water at the same time as watching your favorite comedy clip. It was pure shock and it was pure adrenalin.

The entire team rose out of their seats, shouting, pumping the air, with tears streaming down their faces. They danced around the cabin, grabbed each other by the shoulders and hugged. Held each other tight.

This is family, Drake thought. *This is what every man and woman fights to find their entire lives. This . . . is gold.*

It took a long time to calm everyone down and by then the

signal was fluctuating. Yorgi told them he couldn't be moved for a while and that they would have to fly over to see him. He told them he'd been shot twice and had survived only due to Webster's and Archer's heroic efforts to keep him alive by distracting the mercenaries who'd been sent to kill him.

He told them poignantly that it was the second time he'd survived death in those frozen wastes. Cambridge's call earlier had been made in haste, prompted by one over-eager medic that hadn't checked Yorgi properly at that point, or figured out that the ice fields would have slowed his pulse.

Drake gave him the bad news about their friends, about Luka Kovalenko and Devil's Island, and finally asked him to make somebody fetch him a proper satellite phone. Then they could make clearer plans. The phone call ended with many vigorous goodbyes, all of them tinged with the sad knowledge that Smyth and Lauren would never make this same call.

Drake took five minutes to rummage around the cabin, finding tumblers and small miniature whiskeys for everyone.

He sat down. "Let's raise a glass," he said. "One more time for our fallen friends. For everything they accomplished, how they laughed, how they made memories. And for what they believed in."

The team drank and didn't hide their tears. They all shared the same feelings.

"And one more," Drake said. "For Mai, Luther and Karin, our friends lost. We will never rest, never stop searching. We will fight for you every single day until the day we find you."

He emptied the glass. They all did.

Then they got straight to work.

CHAPTER FORTY SIX

Mai and Luther, Karin and Dino sat inside the container as their ship heaved through an unknown ocean.

At first, they had fought captivity. Wrestled with the door. Tried to break the mechanism, anything to jam it open. They had sought other means of escape, testing the steel itself and the welded joints at all four corners. They had looked to the ceiling and the floor. Searched every inch for a weapon, a makeshift crowbar, an object they could turn into an escape device.

Of course, there was nothing. Their captors were professionals, compelled by the deadliest man they'd ever encountered. They told their captors as much when, on occasion, they brought fresh food and water. These started out as escape opportunities, but it soon became clear that any attempt would get at least one of them badly hurt or killed.

There was always a man with a camera, filming everything that happened.

Alone, the four made plans and took stock of everything they had. A bare light bolted to the right side of the container. Four blankets. Overlarge sweaters. Boxes of biscuits and confectionary. Bottles of water. Cans of soda. Five buckets, one full of fresh water, and a bar of soap. At first, the rolling seas upset them, but they became used to it. Keeping track of passing days was hard but they knew they'd been at sea for at least three.

So far.

The ship's progress felt slow to Mai. It rolled and listed, and seemed to float for an age. She tried to engage with their captors and failed.

The next day, Dino tried. He failed too. No information was offered. They were not treated to any comforts, but they were treated fairly.

"I guess we're here for the long run," Luther said one night. Mai thought it was their fourth.

"We should save our energy," Karin said. "For what's on the other side of this voyage."

"Not much choice," Luther grumbled.

Mai pulled a blanket over her legs, feeling the seeping cold of an ocean night settling in. "We're a long way from DC," she said.

"And from everywhere," Dino put in. "Just sayin'."

"You don't know that," Luther told him. "We could be sailing around and around the Caribbean."

It raised a smile, which was the whole point. Mai pulled the blanket higher and moved closer to the big man. On the other side of the container she saw Karin and Dino do the same. It might be this shared, deadly experience, it might be nothing more than proximity, but Mai already knew Luther was a good man at heart.

She felt drawn to him now.

She saw Karin snuggling in to Dino. The Italian-American closed his eyes and hugged her tight.

Mai grabbed Luther's right arm and held on.

"You think we have something?" he asked, turning.

"I think there's a chance," she said, "which is most unlike me. But I don't normally date. I know when a man is right for me."

"And that humbles me right away."

"It should. It's a very short list."

"So all we have to do is escape Devil's Island and we're on?"

"On?"

"Dating, you know."

"I don't date either, Luther. I am either in a real relationship or I'm not. Can you handle that?"

"I believe that I can and want to give it a try."

Mai held on and together, they rode out the ups and downs of the ocean, trapped for now but ready for action.

They would know when the boat docked. They would know when the time was right.

Karin and Dino fell asleep in each other's arms, chatting, reminiscing, swopping old stories of Wu—the friend that they had lost—almost admitting the love they felt for each other but not quite spanning that bridge.

Mai and Luther held each other tight too, thinking about the bond growing between them, but not mentioning it aloud again.

It wouldn't do to tempt fate.

<u>THE END</u>

<u>For more information on the future of the Matt Drake world and other David Leadbeater novels please read on:</u>

I do hope you enjoyed THE BLOOD KING LEGACY. I must say, the deaths were as hard to write as they were to read. This book forms the start of a new phase for the SPEAR team. The whole scenario will change, giving the books a fresh outlook, with the chance for more diverse adventures. Next up, *Devil's Island* (due January 2019), will play out the current adventure and then Drake 21 (due mid-2019) will introduce some exciting new developments. All part of Hayden's 'proposition'.
Can't wait for you to read the new stuff!

If you enjoyed this book, please leave a review.

Other Books by David Leadbeater:

The Matt Drake Series
A constantly evolving, action-packed romp based in the
escapist action-adventure genre:

The Bones of Odin (Matt Drake #1)
The Blood King Conspiracy (Matt Drake #2)
The Gates of Hell (Matt Drake 3)
The Tomb of the Gods (Matt Drake #4)
Brothers in Arms (Matt Drake #5)
The Swords of Babylon (Matt Drake #6)
Blood Vengeance (Matt Drake #7)
Last Man Standing (Matt Drake #8)
The Plagues of Pandora (Matt Drake #9)
The Lost Kingdom (Matt Drake #10)
The Ghost Ships of Arizona (Matt Drake #11)
The Last Bazaar (Matt Drake #12)
The Edge of Armageddon (Matt Drake #13)
The Treasures of Saint Germain (Matt Drake #14)
Inca Kings (Matt Drake #15)
The Four Corners of the Earth (Matt Drake #16)
The Seven Seals of Egypt (Matt Drake #17)
Weapons of the Gods (Matt Drake #18)

The Alicia Myles Series
Aztec Gold (Alicia Myles #1)
Crusader's Gold (Alicia Myles #2)
Caribbean Gold (Alicia Myles #3)

The Torsten Dahl Thriller Series
Stand Your Ground (Dahl Thriller #1)

The Relic Hunters Series
The Relic Hunters (Relic Hunters #1)
The Atlantis Cipher (Relic Hunters #2)

The Disavowed Series:
The Razor's Edge (Disavowed #1)
In Harm's Way (Disavowed #2)
Threat Level: Red (Disavowed #3)

The Chosen Few Series
Chosen (The Chosen Trilogy #1)
Guardians (The Chosen Tribology #2)

Short Stories
Walking with Ghosts (A short story)
A Whispering of Ghosts (A short story)

All genuine comments are very welcome at:

davidleadbeater2011@hotmail.co.uk

Twitter: @dleadbeater2011

Visit David's website for the latest news and information:
davidleadbeater.com